ELEVATION
OF
MANA

✧ BOOK 2 ✧

ELEVATION OF MANA

✦ BOOK 2 ✦

WANDERING AGENT

Podium

Published in 2024 by Podium Publishing
www.podiumaudio.com

ELEVATION
OF
MANA
✧ BOOK 2 ✧

CHAPTER 1

THE DANGERS OF WATER

Tunderstand you have questions," I said to Shorin. "I hope that I can
assuage them for you."

"As do I, though the biggest of which is, *why*?" he replied, looking
up from the small cup of what passed for tea here. I noted that both
the cup and the pot it had been poured from came from my supplied
pieces and wondered what they were using before.

"*Why*? Surely you can see the uses for what I propose?"

"I do. A flowing . . . pipe of water is certainly something to look
into, but we have always done things one way; to change them now
would be too much." He was cautious, not objecting, which was good.

"This project won't actually change much, sir, since someone will
have to manually supply the water that goes in; but it will serve as proof
that it can be done. Think of it like practice—to first show that a spear
can be thrown, don't you have to try it? You wouldn't take it hunting
without practicing first."

He leaned in. "Ah, I like that, but it does lead to another question.
What are you hunting here that you need to try out your spear?"

I had to admit that he had me there. I'd practically admitted that I
was aiming for bigger and better things. Was his caution born of thinking this new idea might be dangerous, or was it because he wondered

what I might do with it in the future? I needed to assuage both of his concerns if we were to proceed.

"You know what the city smells like in the dry season? When the weather is warm and there's no rain to wash away all of the . . . excess buildup. No matter how hard you try, you can't stop some people from leaving a mess, but something like this could help. We could make it easy for places to get rid of all that waste and wash it away from Atal."

"Is there truly no other reason?" he inquired, seemingly in disbelief.

"No? Why should there be?"

"Ah, sometimes I see the things you do and forget just how young you are, Justin," the elder said with a shake of his head. "Young people like you so often forget the astounding power of water and the good it can bring."

"Is that not what I'm trying to bring to Atal though?" I asked.

"No. Young Justin, I have lived here a very, very long time. Have you ever seen a river overflow from its banks to consume a village? Ever seen the ocean rise and overtake a city? There have been close calls, you know; times when only fast action saved even Atal. Water, young man, is cruel and potent."

For a time I sat, thinking on what he was saying. When I was a boy, the elder of my village had felt similarly about fire. That made sense; since we lived in a forest, fire was an extreme threat. Here though, fire would be less so. A river passed through the city itself, and with so many potent users of magic, fires could be easily taken care of. A tidal wave though? Or a flood? What about a storm surge? Here in Atal, water might be considered by the elders to be the threat, and they would be right.

"I do not anticipate that we will ever be using that much in the city," I started before thinking deeper and stammering a bit. "Not anytime soon at least."

"What are you thinking of for right now?" he asked, a gleam in his eye.

Dams had appeared in my mind unbidden. They were structures that could abate the sort of thing he was concerned with, and without much issue. There were some truly massive structures on Earth—Hoover in the U.S. and Three Gorges in China were the first to come to mind—but even smaller dams would cause incredible chaos if they failed.

"There might be ways to store that much water up, but it would take a long time, and it would be nothing like what I'm proposing. Even then, we wouldn't want something like that here in Atal," I said, not truly answering his question.

Shorin leaned back, rubbing his chin. "Interesting, so what would happen if one of these pipes of yours burst? How bad could it be?"

"Well, a street could flood, but it shouldn't be any worse than that, and even that would be something we could fix before trying to build the entire thing," I answered.

"Hmm, I'll want to see how you would prevent them before we go beyond your test. For now though, let us discuss supplies and how to actually build it."

Over the next hour or two I went into detail about how many bricks I would need, how many people, how long it would take, and all the other gritty details. Then I was told to wait. My project here might be smaller than a full, city-wide plan, but it would still need to be brought before the leaders of the city. Overall, it wasn't the worst answer I could have gotten.

Shorin

I watched as the youngling left my home. He wasn't a boy; not truly, but every year people seemed younger and younger to me. It made me chuckle when I thought how my own ancestor must view us. Perhaps I too was very, very young and naive.

He didn't understand though; not truly. At his age he'd never seen a stream that had been diverted carve a canyon in only a few years, or the enormous waves that even the strongest in the city struggled to protect us from. On the other hand, that gleam in his eye when he thought about destruction, and how he avoided explaining. Little Justin had ideas on how to weaponize water; that was something I knew would be worth the hassle.

"I don't know; what do you think?" I asked the servant girl who came to refill my drink.

Her eyes flicked around the otherwise empty room for a moment. "M-me, sir?" she asked.

"Is there anyone else here?"

I let my eyes flick down to the markings on her, which that told me just how long she would have to work for me; years and years yet remained on her time. She didn't know it, but she was a distant relative, one whose contract I'd purchased using income from that lad's inventions. It was better for her here, as I could see to it she wouldn't be mistreated. Some people were truly horrible to their servants. If I could mold her into something useful in the time I had her, though, I might even tell her of our kinship when it was over.

"I . . . don't know. I'm not sure I completely understand. It sounds like he has a good idea, but since I've never seen anything like what he's suggesting, perhaps use caution?" Her voice rose at the end, more a question than an answer.

A small laugh escaped me, and the tension in her muscles eased. "If more youths thought like that, we'd have a lot more elders. Now off with you; I'm sure you've other duties."

CHAPTER 2

WORKSHOP

After leaving Shorin to his business, I headed home. I hadn't moved from the first place I'd bought; though I had purchased some of the surrounding houses when my money flow came back, and I made a few . . . improvements. No longer was my home a single small dwelling, but now a complex to rival even Shorin's, with a few buildings surrounding a large courtyard.

When I returned, Chien went to one of his work spaces. I'd set up a few small shop rooms with basic equipment for him. He needed space to practice what I was teaching him if he was to teach others, particularly as things got more and more complicated. The kid was a magnificent worker, and more than once, I'd considered teaching him more about magic. But, I held back; the understanding I possessed of some magical principles could make someone far too powerful.

While he tinkered, I turned to a rather smooth-looking portion of wall and reached out with my magic. The operation was delicate and had to be done manually, but soon enough a door formed, and I descended into the real heart of my home. If Shorin had ever been down here, he would have lost his mind. The things above ground were valuable to others, but the things down here were valuable to me.

A series of oil lamps—the elves already had a prototype—lit the space and shined light upon my real work. There was more than copper or iron here; I had samples of everything from aluminum to tungsten, painstakingly isolated and purified from every sample I could get my hands on. Most of them were useless for now, but I needed some for very specific applications, and making them was fun.

My real project, though, sat on a massive stone table. It was a mixture of what I'd seen as a human and what I thought must be possible from this world. This would one day be a wonderful addition to what we all could do, if I could get it to work.

People in this world had tattoos created with magical inks that somehow interfaced with them, slightly boosting their abilities. They were considered a go-to for certain professionals who didn't have a particular magical skill set and needed small boosts, and they proved a point—magic could interface with people who weren't casters like me. Anyone with a bit of power and some training could focus their magic into an area, and it would respond.

That sounded to me like an input, a very basic one, but input nonetheless. In my former life I'd been researching computers, and in this life I might just make something better than I'd ever imagined. I was going to create a magical computer, something that could catapult this society straight into the information age. Well, if I could ever figure it out, that is.

Before me sat a basic counting machine, one that didn't work. I'd made it from available materials that would work with electricity though, so I had to manually power it. The theory was solid, but still it wouldn't function. It wasn't supposed to do much, just keep a number and add one to it repeatedly—a simple process really, something that could be built at home on Earth.

The issue was the materials, of that much I was sure. Magic wasn't electricity, and though it did respond similarly in some situations, they were profoundly different forces. The many materials I'd tested all seemed to dislike conducting it in the way I wanted. I'd even played with a lot of the bases to the magical tattoos, once even putting a basic circuit onto a small captured rodent. None of them worked, and the mouse only sort of glowed—not the reaction I was looking for.

With a sigh, I pulled out a bit of charcoal and reached out with my mind, reforming the paths into a new material. A pulse of will freed the carbon from the slag and left all the impurities behind, and then I began reforming it again.

Magic flowed like an extension of myself, pouring out and over my spell. I didn't need to imagine every single atom and where it would go, only the structure of the thing I imagined and what I wanted it to do. It was like being the conductor of an orchestra; only I didn't need to manage every note, just the song. I could even feel it as the power responded—unseen energy flowing just the way I wanted it to. That sensation was one I'd truly never get tired of.

Sweat began to bloom on my brow as, one by one, a spiraling series of woven carbon nanotubes connected the points in my computer, replacing the wires and other bits one by one. An hour passed, then another, intense concentration never wavering as it all came together. The structure was not hard, no; it was weaving it where it needed to go without breaking it that caused problems.

When it was all done I was drenched in sweat, but I smiled down at my creation. The internal components of my design were all purest black—nearly invisible.

"Come now, my sweet; let's see what you can do," I said as I pushed the smallest amount of magic into my computer.

There was a tiny flash, and I watched in horror as my work disintegrated before my eyes. It was hard to determine the exact problem, but whatever it was cascaded through the whole thing like falling dominoes, leaving nothing behind but sooty residue.

With a wave, I gathered up the now useless carbon. "How's it go? Now I know a thousand ways that don't work?" I mused as I told the carbon to make a diamond.

The little crystal formed in my hand without any real effort. It was a repeating structure with no changes needed, no angles or turns, I didn't even care the shape it formed. That made it all the easier, as it seemed repeating structures loved to form.

"Maybe I'm going about this the wrong way? Perhaps magical materials are needed, not more mundane ones?"

As I thought out loud, I began to make cuts in my newly formed stone, trying to make it look like the advertisements I'd seen on Earth. It wouldn't be a good one and, in fact, would probably horrify anyone who worked in the industry, but it's not like anyone cared here. This little trinket wouldn't even be leaving my lab anytime soon.

"It's a shame diamond doesn't work for currency; it's pretty though," I said to myself. It had been one of my earlier tests. "Well, counting machine, let's try again later."

There was still so much on my plate. I needed to go check on the metal Chien had told me was on its way to me and begin using it to make product. There was a waiting list a mile long already; everyone wanted something made of metal. The highest calls were for simple tools like blades and hammers, some of which could be made in bulk and at speed.

Musing done, I tossed the little diamond in a drawer and left my lab. There was always more to do, always so much more. Perhaps one day I'd be able to take a vacation.

CHAPTER 3

CUSTOMER COMPLAINT

Chien stood by as I worked in my shop. I poured more and more of my mana into the fire as the copper began to melt, knowing that the little crucible formed of magical force could take it.

"The men selling this should be beaten," I declared, not even fully done yet.

"Okay . . . why?"

"See all the black stuff forming on the liquid there? Those are impurities, and this copper is loaded with them. It's like they didn't even try to make it pure, just got it good enough," I griped.

"Well, you know, Justin, it's not like everyone knows that. Maybe they'd never made it before," the young man argued.

"If it were something they'd made, or they were actually working the material, I could live with that, Chien, but they're selling it bulk; it's just unprofessional." Something pinged in the back of my mind, and I smiled. "Should make a complaint, make them the next Ea-nāṣir."

"The what?"

"A man who sold shoddy copper; don't worry about it."

"Right . . ."

I don't think Chien believed me, but my assistant was oddly willing to let a lot of things slide, so long as I kept giving him profitable work. "So, why am I here?" he asked.

"To learn what we're looking for. I won't always be around to get supplies, and frankly, there aren't many people I'd trust to do it for me," I answered.

"I'm touched you'd put that much trust in me."

I looked back to see him with a hand on his chest and what might have been the most sarcastic face I'd ever seen. "Starved for options here, Chien," I quipped. "Regardless, you do good work."

Before we could continue, there came a knock at the door. Since I was clearly busy, Chien went to answer it and came back with one of my other few friends in tow, who was scowling. No matter what I did, those two still didn't like each other, which was understandable. Chien and Ian were just too different. That said, they at least kept the bickering to a minimum around me.

"Ian, wasn't expecting you today," I said as he joined us in the shop. We weren't doing anything secret, or even all that interesting to most people, so it was fine if he came into the shop.

"To be honest, I wasn't expecting to be here either," he replied. "Heard you got more copper, though, and came to see if all of it was spoken for."

"Most of it, yes. Is there something specific you need?" I inquired. In order for me to keep things going as they were, I had to keep Ian and his grandfather happy.

"Well, I was hoping I might be able to get a spear, but I know they're pretty expensive . . ."

"Why a spear?" I asked, a little curious about the use.

Copper spears were good, in many ways better than stone. They lasted longer, were sharper, and tended to pierce things a lot more effectively. That being said, most of the time it wasn't worth the cost. It was a lot of material, and unless you had a lot of copper, liked to show off, or really needed a top-tier weapon, it wasn't worth it.

"It might seem silly, but I feel as if I need to get serious. Most of my siblings are already in better positions than myself, and I need something to . . . help me along the route," he explained, dejected. "I'm good at my job, but I lack the power. I don't have the kind of fire you two do."

Ian was short on magic; that much was true. Much like my childhood friend Ninden, he could boost his strength very briefly, but it ended there. He simply lacked the magic for much else.

"A tattoo?" I suggested, knowing that having one would give him another ability, but he shook his head.

"Sadly, that won't work. No matter how hard I train, I'm just not getting much stronger at any appreciable rate. I even asked my grandfather; he said it would come with time, but . . ."

But this world was harsh. He didn't need to say it. The reason elders were respected and cared for was just that. The city was safer, true, but even here there were monster attacks every now and then, and the guards had to go and deal with them, power or not. Perhaps his would grow over time. In my experience, all elves that lived long enough gained some magic, but sometimes the wait was long.

I looked him over. Ian and I didn't end up working together very often, but he was always around and a good liaison between me and some of the powers of the city. Perhaps I could introduce him to something new.

"I don't think a spear is what you need," I told him. "A spear would only make you a little better at hurting things, but something to protect you might do more than that."

"I have a shield already," he retorted.

He was right. Shields were common and normally made of wicker or wood. They were such an obvious idea that really anyone looking for a fight could have come up with them quickly. The same went for armor. It existed, but it was poorly made—nothing more than bits of bone and wood tied to cover the wearer's arms and legs.

"I've got some ideas if you're willing to trust me. Let me think and work on some things, and I'll see what I can come up with. The copper is still expensive, though, so be ready for that," I told him.

"Sure," he said.

I blinked at him for a few moments. There was still slag settling atop my current batch of ore, and after hastily using magic to scrape it to the side, I stopped heating it completely.

"What?" he asked.

"You accepted that too easily," I said.

"Oh, I know most people think you're mad, Justin, but your work works." He smiled at me, shaking his head. "Like your pipe idea . . . a few of my grandfather's advisors are worried it'll collapse, but I'm betting you've already thought of that."

"Yeah, it's an arch," I answered, and both Ian and Chien gave me a blank look. We really needed to institute some basic skills education one day. It's something I couldn't do, but it was needed. "The shape— it's called an arch."

They both had no idea what I was talking about, so after that batch of copper cooled I got some bricks for a demonstration. Arches were so simple, and so key to building things that it shocked me I'd never thought of it. They were right there, a low-hanging fruit that everyone could use. Heck, even people in villages could build these for bridges and the like.

Chien seemed to think the design was neat, but not really something he could use day to day. Ian, on the other hand, was looking at it intently as I jumped atop the small structure I'd built so I could explain better. He worked all around the city, so as I spoke, I watched him, and I could see him thinking. Thinking was good, thinking built societies.

CHAPTER 4

ARMOR 101

Unsurprisingly, a couple of days after my conversation with Ian, I obtained full approval to build the first section of sewers for the city. I knew he'd told his grandfather what I'd said and had maybe even given him a demonstration. That was fine; this first sewer line would only connect Shorin's house and a few other places to a river bed not far outside the city wall, but it would serve as an artery that could then be expanded upon when the powers that be realized how well it worked.

That, of course, led to other problems, like the ones I was dealing with now. Even if the section I was building was small—much smaller than a full system, and simple—it still required materials. There were a lot of different people paying for the endeavor, myself included. That alone wasn't too bad, as labor was cheap, but it still had to be organized.

Luckily, brick-making was already on the rise in Atal, the technology having been spread by Chien and myself a while ago. It was still small in scope, but there were a few groups of men who'd taken it up; they weren't proper businesses yet, but one day they might be. I stood back and watched Chien, letting him explain to the gathered workers exactly what we wanted.

The bricks we were using were oddly shaped—one side wider than the other rather than the standard rectangle, which is what we needed to aid the formation of the arches. I could have brought in cement for this, but that would only have complicated things further; this first part needed to be as simple as possible. Later iterations could be more complex.

When he was finished, he returned to my side. I'd chosen well with this lad; he'd done all right so far. He'd managed to take my explanations, make them his own, and get others working. Something I didn't have the time for and didn't really want to do.

"You know this is going to take like, years, right?" he asked as we walked away from the worksite.

"That's fine," I replied. "With the amount of materials we need . . . Unless we conscripted hundreds of people, it was always going to. I also noticed the spellcasters in their group, so once they really get going, I think it'll proceed well."

"You use the strangest terms. 'Spellcaster,' like the power is what's important," he said with a shake of his head.

"It is to me. We need to have designated words for such things, and we need to have discussions about the power of magic too. If everyone is going to use their own words for things, I will as well. Making it clear that I'm not talking about actual fire or lightning is important."

"Whatever. Anyway, what's next for us?" he asked.

"What do you mean?"

"You're always up to something new. I wanna know what's next, like that stuff you told Ian you'd think about. What's that?"

That was something I'd been contemplating for a while now—effective armor. While for some of us it wouldn't make sense, for others it would be a lifesaver. The question wasn't how to make effective armor; the question was how to make it without using a massive amount of metal. That one had kept pinging around in my head for days.

There were only so many means of protection in my previous world, and only so many in this one. Weight, flexibility, durability, and repair ability all came into the equations and had their limits. This meant that I was mostly limited to things like cloth or metal, or perhaps hardened leather, though I knew that the latter might pose issues during the rainy season.

"There are a few ways we could build something to protect him, but my concern is where we'd get the stuff to do it," I answered.

"I mean, you just make most stuff, so can't you just make it?"

"I could . . . but there would be problems." That answer was true enough, in that displaying a new metal would bring massive issues.

"What sort of stuff would you need?" he asked.

Having someone to bounce ideas off of was always a blessing, so I began to list things out. "Light material, if possible, easy to make, and durable."

"What about pottery?" he asked, making me smile.

Ceramics had been used in some armors on Earth, primarily for ballistic armor. Perhaps there was some form that might work, but I didn't have it.

"What we have now is too fragile; it would break, or be too heavy. Good for protecting buildings maybe, like bricks, but not a person."

"Leather, like really thick?"

"I'm sure people have thought of it, and up to a point, it could work, but what about when it rains?" If our climate was European, perhaps we could use wax to fix it, make it harder, but we were in a tropical climate; it would be a mess.

"Hmm, not like he's a snail or something and can grow his own."

That made me stop for a moment and think. A snail wouldn't work, no; too small and curved, but shell? There were a lot of different kinds of shells, and they're hard and light, and we lived right by the bleeding ocean, so there were always plenty. The small pretty shells used as money were only one type, but others, which were considered less useful, were everywhere. Heck, I had already gathered a few in my experiments with making my own lime, so I knew how available it was.

"Chien, you're brilliant," I exclaimed.

"Oh, yeah I know, but about what?"

"Let's go to the shore."

"Wait, about what?" he repeated as I began walking.

The young man trailed after me, continuing his questions about a number of my ideas, but I mostly lost myself in going through my memories. We'd need to find the right kind of shell, and then shape them. Yeah, this could work. I just needed to figure out the connections, and those shouldn't be too hard.

Before I knew it I was at the shore, looking over several pieces of thick shell. These came from a local species of abalone. They made up a portion of the city's shellfish and were well liked. They were also huge, with parts of their shell more than big enough for me to make a few small plates.

"Yeah, these will do nicely," I said.

"Little small, huh?" Chien said. "I mean, Ian's a big guy; not sure how you're planning to fit him into one."

"Not one, many." I put one of the shells in the water, since I didn't fancy breathing in seashell dust, and began to cut it with my magic.

It didn't take long. The sort of physical manipulation used here was among my favorite spells. I sliced the shell into a few bits, around an inch and a half by three inches. I didn't have any specific memories of how lamellar had been connected, but after a few quick drawings, I had a layout I thought might work. A quick drilling spell, much like I used on woodwork, and I had a few plates to play with.

Chien stood back. "You know, I always see your results, Justin, but watching you come up with crazy ideas as you go is wild. Do you actually think this will work?"

"Yes, yes I do."

CHAPTER 5

ARMOR 201

It was easy to stand back and admire my work, the satisfaction of a job . . . Well, I wasn't yet sure how well it had been done. Things seemed to be going well, but really the whole reason I was here was to check on my work in action.

In the courtyard, Ian and a friend of his were sparring, spears flashing forward at speed. These, of course, were training weapons, and not properly sharp, but they felt like the real thing, and the guards liked to practice with them. While the other guard was wearing little more than the leather clothing so common in Atal, my friend was covered in a few simple pieces of armor, the lamellar plates cracking once as he was struck.

"How's it feel?" I asked as the two finished up.

"Not bad, but there's definitely some movement restriction," Ian answered. "Parts of the back just aren't bending like they should, and I think the front is too wide in places. I can fight, but it's not great."

"Luckily, some of that is easy to fix," I responded, looking where he'd indicated.

I wasn't surprised, as even getting it to this point had been a chore. Never before had I made armor, so there were things I just didn't know. The human—or in this case, elven—body wasn't flat; it needed to bend and twist, particularly around the limbs, and armor hindered that movement. Perhaps I could never get it perfect, but I could at least make it better.

"The real question is, will it protect him?" Ian's friend asked.

"I brought a few plates with me," I said. "Why don't we set them up and test?" I anticipated this to be the next step. Preparedness kept people from doing foolish things, like testing the armor while wearing it or draping it over something else.

The extra pieces I'd brought were about a foot in width and length and were made the same way as the armor. We quickly added them to one of the practicing posts—a wattle fence made out of woven rushes. Then the striking began.

First, spears were thrown at the armor piece, and then stabbed into it. The men involved seemed to like these tests, and soon other weapons made of wood and stone were brought into the equation. Knives and small blades did little, as expected, and the armor even held up well against heavier weapons like clubs and hammers. One by one, guards came and laid into it, pieces chipping and breaking a bit, but never fully shattering.

"Holds up," one of the guardsmen commented with a nod. "At least to normal stuff."

There was a collective smile as more weapons were brought to the fore. This time the actions were repeated, but with significantly more power. Men used their small amounts of magic to hurl or stab into the armor, and the damage soon began to show.

I was still pretty satisfied; my creation held up well until the first wooden club impacted it. Even then, two clubs broke, with much of the force involved dissipating into the environment and making the clubs shatter rather than the target itself.

We all stood back, each taking our turn to look at the destruction.

"I want one," came the voice of the man who'd been fighting Ian earlier.

"Should work against those not using their power, and even lesser beasts. Probably wouldn't do much for a stronger one, but even then, it might save your life," another agreed.

I was looking over the damage to all of the weapons. Most of them had been destroyed because the blades were just too weak. A stone blade was rather poor at holding an edge, the sharpened end prone to shattering. It looked like most of the spears and knives had done just that. If you got hit with a hammer or something, your ribs would probably still break, but it looked like even some of those weapons were no match for the armor until the real strength had been brought to the fight.

In the end, my testing plate was broken, but parts of it could be salvaged. That was one of the benefits of this kind of armor—even if it failed, not all of it was gone. I could easily take the remaining plates and reuse them. Some might be a little weaker, but that was probably fine . . .

"So, what are you selling them for?" one of the guards asked me.

"No clue yet; need a better source of materials," I explained, trying to avoid their hungry eyes.

"Well if you need help . . ." Ian began.

"Yeah, I'd like one of those idiots out west to start something." That was an odd comment from one of the assembled warriors, and my look must have alerted him.

"Rumor has it they're doing a lot of training and moving around. Nothing concrete, but Atal and their ancient don't get along," he said with a shrug.

"None of the ancients get along," one of them said with a shake of his head.

"Hate to break it to you, but even that armor won't save you if an ancient decides you need to die," Ian added.

"Never said it would, but against another soldier, maybe." They went back and forth for a while, each having their own opinion on the matter.

Something about that pricked my nerves; my family lived in the west. Perhaps I could send them a message. If I couldn't return myself, I could send word and tell them they could come to Atal. There was no postal service or anything of the kind in this world, but if I caught a merchant heading that way, I could get him to carry word to them. I even knew a few that ran that route, all very interested in copper.

Hands and body continuing their work, my thoughts remained on that track for quite a while. It wasn't until we all split that someone spoke to me.

"You okay?" Ian asked as he walked beside me.

"Yeah, why?" I tripped, not sure what I'd hit for a moment.

"Because you just stepped in a bush," he said, laughing.

I tried to extricate myself. "Just thinking about home, after what they said about the troubles in the west. Is there that much of a problem?" I asked as I pulled myself from the branches and leaves.

Ian thought for a moment. "Things are different out there. The land rises into valleys and mountains, and that's where Atal's territory ends. On the other side of them though things are different. It's very flat and very dry, there are few large trees, and the beasts are different. Well, at least that's what my grandfather says, but I don't think he's actually even been over there."

"Maybe if they're getting restless I should send for my family," I mused, wanting his opinion.

"Might be a risk either way. Travel is dangerous, but I don't think anything will happen for a few years yet. Ancients move slow most of the time. Even if they're restless, why would they harm anyone in a small village? Not much out there but woods and trees."

"Maybe . . . I'll see if I can find a messenger though," I said, not willing to inform him that there was at least one odd thing there. But it was probably best not to say anything about the massive magical pool that could draw people in from other universes.

CHAPTER 6

BREAK-IN

As I wandered through one of the districts near the market, I griped about the lack of a mail system, or of a written language. At some point someone might have made a written system, but if they had, I'd yet to discover it. It would make things so much easier, but most people didn't seem to care one way or the other.

I could make my own written language, but I feared it would go the same way as farming. People would understand it, but most wouldn't care. After all, if your memory was perfect, why would you need to write things down? Perhaps if I gained enough notoriety I could press the issue, but for now I just had to stew.

There were problems like I had now, but some of those came down to inexperience, at least in the minds of the common people. I was looking for a particular merchant, Orran, but I was unsure of exactly where he lived. There weren't addresses after all, and I'd never been to his house, so trying to find him was a pain.

It took me a fair part of the day, but eventually I found someone who was happy to lead me to his home. The cost of a few of the smaller shell beads that everyone used was insignificant in comparison to the amount of time it would save me, and soon, I found myself in front of his place.

The house itself was rather normal. There were two stories, the bottom made from the stone common in the area, while the top was, like mine, formed out of a living tree with magic and divided into multiple living quarters. There were, of course, some stark differences between our homes. Unlike my house, Orran's was formed with several others around a little central square, almost like a cul-de-sac, the common area opening onto the street.

My approach was noticed by more than one person, with several peeking through their windows or doors, trying to find out what I was doing as I walked up to the door. There was no news here, so gossip was always popular, and being that I was clearly someone they didn't know . . .

Before I even reached the door to knock or call out, it was opened by a woman who appeared frozen at the same age we all seemed to end up at. She had mousy brown hair pulled back over her ears and uncompromising eyes. Behind her, with a head barely reaching her waist, was a child holding onto her leg, who I assumed was hers.

"Do you need something?" she asked rather curtly.

"Yes, I'm looking for a traveling merchant, Orran?" I replied.

"He's not here right now; what do you need?" Again, she seemed none too pleased to be talking to me.

"A message delivered to one of the villages on his normal route. Any idea when he'll be back?"

"No, who should I tell him came by?" she finally asked with a huff.

I gave her my name, and the general area where I lived, but with her outright hostility, I gave that about a fifty-fifty chance of ever making it to Orran. Hopefully his wife wasn't like that all the time, but if she was, it would easily explain why my contact often went traveling.

I briefly entertained the idea of finding another traveling merchant or runner to deliver my message, but opted against it. Things were probably fine, so there was no need to rush. My family knew where I was anyway, so if they needed me they could probably find some way to contact me.

There were still a few projects I wanted to work on before going to bed, so I headed home, hoping that things would work out.

Later That Night

"You sure this is the place?" one of the men asked as they hid in the shadows of an alley, all looking at a particular building.

"Yeah, one of my cousins listened to him describe it in the merchant district earlier today, and you should have seen the smoke coming off the building when I stopped by earlier. This is definitely the place," their leader confirmed, looking at his two assistants.

"Rumors are the guy's a weirdo, but he's got power. Sure this is a good idea?"

"Listen, that guy works copper, bud. All those pieces in the market, that's him. I also checked around, and it's just him. We do this, and we can all buy anything we want, no problem," the leader answered.

"And if he finds us?" the third asked.

"Three against one, and while surprised? We do what we have to," the leader said, smiling.

As one the three men slipped through a small window, they found it was latched shut. However, long ago, they had worked out how to bypass standard closures. The smallest of the three perked at another sound as they opened it.

"What was that?" he asked.

"What?" the leader whispered back.

"A small tinging, like a bird or something, but not one I know."

"Probably copying something it heard, now be quiet; we don't want to wake this bastard." That made enough sense, as some birds did indeed copy any noise they heard, at times even learning a word or two.

They slipped through the bottom floor, looking around until they finally came to the room they assumed was their target. One wall had several forges constructed against it, while nearby there were a few places for mounting anvils. Stones and benches were everywhere, but the most valuable thing in the room was a few clay bowls.

"Where's the copper?" one of the men asked their boss.

"Fuck, he must have hidden it. Pull everything out," the leader instructed. He knew that sometimes men hid their valuables. If worse came to worst, they could always beat the information out of the owner. That would be difficult since he could use magic and didn't have any hostages handily laying around, but it could still work.

No sooner had he spoken than a small ball of light flitted into the room. The thieves barely had time to register what was going on before it violently exploded into a riot of color and sound, causing each man to grab his ears or cover his eyes.

CHAPTER 7

JUSTICE

As my alarm spell went off, I thought it odd that no one had attempted to rob me sooner. Coming from my previous world, I understood I was now quite well off, and how people would want some of that wealth, but I was surprised it had taken so long to get to this point.

Over the years, I'd played with multiple setups for protecting my stuff, but this was the first I knew of that it had been needed. Originally, I had just kept everything put away, which I still did, of course, but now I had little strings on all my entry points that rang bells in my room should anything happen. That had been the alert that someone had broken into my house, rousing me from sleep and bringing me to check on these idiots.

The spell stopped, and I stepped into the doorway. The flashbangs worked. The three men trying to pick themselves up off the ground were a good example of this.

"Fuck, get him!" one of them shouted, pointing several feet to my left.

They'd come at night, and that meant they were clearly up to no good, so I didn't really bother holding back. The speaker was the first to rise, and he caught a blast of force to the stomach, launching him ass over end into a wall beside the furnace.

The other two were now trying to stand, but were clearly out of it. More bolts of force would be the answer here as well, the small spell spinning up in my hand without much effort. The second of the thieves tried to dodge, jumping up, but that didn't work. I cringed in pain as the bolt that had been heading for number two's midsection instead caught his knee, turning it in a completely unnatural direction. The final man was sent flying from my attack, hitting a wall and slumping like a sack of flour.

I was ready to tie them up and call for the guards. At least that's what I thought. Out of the corner of my eye, I caught the image of the first thief rising and launching himself at me. Even after the flashbang and being thrown across the room, he still had that much strength and resilience, and I was surprised.

I barely managed to turn in time—a knife he'd brought slipped across my stomach and left a bright red trail rather than gutting me. The flint may have been brittle, but it was still sharp and more than capable of killing me. I needed to stop playing around with these three and end it.

With a hiss of pain, I decided to go back to one of my old favorites— fire. "Very well," I said as I backed up.

There was a brief look of confusion on the thief's face at my words, and then I brought my hands together. As I did I noticed several markings across his skin light up and shine a dull silver, some kind of protective ability. I wondered briefly if it would be enough to save him, then I decided it didn't matter that much.

The lance of fire I shot forward caught him square in the chest, and unlike I intended, didn't go straight through him. Instead, the man was picked up by the blast and hurled backward through a window, and right out into the street.

I didn't want to be caught unaware again, so I turned. The thief with the broken knee was still down, screaming in pain, his friend still unconscious. I didn't have a good way to knock the second guy out, but I did hit him with another force bolt, just to make sure, before heading into the street after the remaining assailant.

He was still kicking. This guy even got up after taking that blast, and I had to admit, I was a little impressed. Sure, his chest was covered in burns, and he looked to be struggling as I hopped through my destroyed window, but he was still quite alive.

Just as I was readying to finish this, we were joined by others. The series of lights and explosions had not gone unnoticed. At the end of the street, several men with spears were drawing nearer. Their outfits spoke of their profession as city guards, and they looked displeased.

My opponent tried to run, but there would be none of that. Had they caught me unaware or asleep, perhaps these men could have hurt me, but I was neither of those things. Planes of force snapped into being around the would-be thief, locking him in a small cell.

"HALT!" came a shout from my side, and I raised my hands, showing that I didn't want to fight.

The guards quickly came up to us and approached me hesitantly. It was clear that I was the one slinging spells, and for a few short moments, I could feel them preparing to fight. They made sure to spread out, one always out of my line of sight, so that someone would be able to strike if I did.

Then one of them produced a light and got a look at my face. After that, things got a lot easier. I was well acquainted with the local law enforcement, and they with me. Because of our perfect memories, they also easily recognized where I was—outside my home. The guards of Atal knew everyone in the districts they patrolled, so explaining myself wasn't too hard.

Quickly the thieves found themselves tied with coarse ropes, and the guards began inspecting everything. They noted the injuries to all of us, looking particularly displeased at the slice on my stomach, as well as the damage done to my house. From there, I was asked to join them while one of them waited at my home.

That, of course, was less a request than an order, so I happily went. I'd done nothing wrong, so there was little worry, but that worry grew as we moved through the city. Step by step we headed toward the biggest of the avenues that led inward. Houses got slightly bigger, slightly nicer, and one building began to loom over all others.

Seeing my concern, one of the guards spoke. "The ancestor likes to hold court at sunrise. When we get there we'll speak, tell him what happened. You'll get a chance to speak, but afterward, don't say anything unless he addresses you. Atal doesn't speak much for these, except to hand down his judgment."

"He'll judge the case himself?" I asked, surprised.

"Things like this are uncommon; theft is one thing, trying to kill someone another. You'll be fine, so long as the ancestor doesn't take offense." He patted me on the shoulder, trying to be reassuring.

Darkness gave way to the pink dawn as we entered and were led to a large opening. The inside of the room was vast, and there were only a few others waiting. Some of those in line were held by guards or tied, and some still could move. Regardless of their status, all seemed on edge.

The room itself was large, squarish, and open. Windows lined the sides, though there were also small fire pits here and there for extra light, a path of them lining a particular approach. Everything was organized around a large stone throne, currently sitting empty on a small dais above everyone and everything else.

As the first golden ray shone through one of the windows, a figure walked lazily through a back door. His hair hung over his shoulders in a silver waterfall. Guards and others in the hall bowed slightly as he passed them and sat upon his throne.

He looked sort of bored as the first pair of petitioners were brought before him. I didn't catch the whole explanation, but it appeared that the two were brothers who were arguing over a house that they'd inherited. That normally wouldn't have been a major thing, but their argument had spilled into the street and caused a large fight among the residents of the neighborhood.

"Tear down the house," Atal declared to one of the guards standing by, looking uninterested. Both men were stunned, but quickly left, not wanting any more of the old elf's attention than they'd already received.

All of the cases here were like that, people causing large disturbances or damages. It was also clear that Atal was harsh and couldn't be bothered for most of it. The case before mine was one of murder. The testimonies were given, and it seemed the perpetrator had been caught in the act.

"Execute her," the ancient declared, one hand resting on a fist.

"No!" the elven woman screamed as guards came to pull her away.

She didn't go quietly, instead forming a ball of energy in her hand and launching it at Atal. I wasn't familiar with her spell, but whatever it had been, it seemed to do absolutely nothing as it splashed against the ancient's skin, bursting like a raindrop.

There was a loud crack—similar to a sonic boom—and suddenly he was in front of the offending woman. There was fear in her eyes, and it was intentional. Atal had opted to give her just enough time to understand her error before he reached forward, one hand landing on her shoulder, the other on her throat. What followed was a short scream of pain and a sickening ripping sound as he pulled, separating her head from her body, like a child pulling apart an insect.

Blood spurted everywhere as the ruler of the city returned to his chair. Water was brought by a waiting serving girl, her hands trembling, with which he washed himself briefly before sitting back down. I sort of pitied her, as that particular job must have been terrifying.

Everyone else in the room was silent as the corpse was pulled away, and then it was our turn.

The thieves were on one side, and I on the other as the guards described what they found. Before they could finish, though, the ancient spoke.

"You," he said, pointing to the thief who'd cut me. "You were banished from my city." There was a pause, as if to give the offender a chance to explain.

The man didn't say anything, simply spat on the ground.

"Execute him, feed his body to the fish," was Atal's response.

He was pulled from the room, but went quietly, simply glaring. As he was removed, the guards finished with their observations.

The two remaining thieves were given a chance to speak. The one with the broken knee went first.

"We meant no ill, Ancient. We were merely confused and entered the wrong house," he lied, trying to smile nervously.

The other went for a completely different route. He looked younger, and terrified. "Please have mercy," was all he said.

Then it was my turn. I briefly described how I'd found them in my home and disabled them, keeping things brief.

"Your leg is damaged; it will be cut off," Atal said to the injured thief after brief consideration. "Then, both of you shall become servants for ten years."

My guess was that the man who would soon be crippled would be offered the chance to have his injury healed. Of course, that would come at a cost, meaning he would be kept in servitude longer. Either that or he'd have to struggle with being unable to walk, which was practically a death sentence. Even if it didn't seem like it, I did have to agree that there'd been some mercy to the thief who'd asked for it.

As we prepared to leave, Atal said, "Wait."

"Ancient?" I asked, turning to face him.

"I would speak with you; remain here until this is done."

The only words that passed through my mind were *Oh crap*.

CHAPTER 8

WORK ORDER

I stood where one of the assistants had directed me, waiting for what might be my last day in this world. I didn't know what Atal wanted of me, but I did know that his sense of justice was much like that of the ancient world. Punishments were meted out and rewards given based on what he deemed fair.

There were only a few court proceedings after mine, but plenty of business. A number of people approached, seeking permission for this or that. Several wanted to build new buildings or remove some they owned from the city. One enterprising elf asked to expand the city walls, and I was surprised to say that it was granted, provided he did it himself.

Finally, there were reports brought in. Messengers from various regions came to give a full account on growth and what was going on in their area. It was clear that Atal only really cared about the villages nearest his city.

Through all of these reports I learned at least a few things. There were imports and exports of all sorts of things, and it sounded like some even went to other nations. There were a lot of procedural aspects I picked up on as well, like some of the people addressing the ruler as "Ancient," just as I had, while others called him "Ancestor." From what I could gather,

Atal had sired many children over the years, and they themselves had sired many more, going down the generations several times. It was subtle, but there was clear favoritism going on with Atal's descendants, so little though that some might not even realize it, but it was there.

As lunchtime rolled around, I was relieved that things were winding down. Almost all of the petitions were dealt with, and those left seemed to be the ruler's direct subordinates. Without preamble he rose from his throne, turning and heading where he'd entered from.

"Come, child," he said as he passed me.

I bristled as I followed him deeper into his palace, but he might have a point. Perhaps to him I was like a child, not that that would save me if he got mad, but it was of note. If I made it to his age, would I consider others who are my current age children? I honestly didn't know, but I couldn't discount the possibility.

I was led into a small inner garden, where there were several places to sit around a small table. All seats were empty and my host motioned to one. He sat before I did, clearly marking his status. I noticed that pieces of my work were here as dishes; perhaps he wanted more pottery, or specialty pieces.

As soon as we sat down, a couple of serving girls came to fill the dishes with fresh fruit, juices, and slices of meat. Like many powerful men in history, he surrounded himself with pretty women in scant clothing. For a brief moment, my eyes rested on the one bringing my drink. Her dress was of good quality, but little material, revealing the marks used to measure the time one was kept as a slave; they covered half her body.

"You may have her if you wish," Atal said, his voice gaining an amused inflection. It appeared he'd noticed I was looking.

The girl let out a tiny whimper before I answered. "No, thank you; I have no desire to own another."

There was a small chuckle as he waved everyone else off, sending them back to the edges of the garden. "You are an interesting one, odd, and useful. You're the one who brought copper to my city, and the best worker of it here."

"I . . . thank you, Ancient," I responded. Maybe he wanted something made of copper.

"Not so long ago, I received a knife, one you made." He looked off into the distance, sighing and smiling. "When I was young, I roamed the land, spear in hand, slaying beasts and elves, and all who stood against me. I struggled at times, I came close to death more than once, and I loved it. Yet, as I grew in age and power, things changed. No longer could I use a spear, as many shattered under my strength, but it was fine. I replaced them with the bones of great beasts. Then those too began to shatter under my grip. Do you know what I desire of you?" he said, a small spark growing in his eyes.

"A spear?" I asked.

"A weapon, boy, a weapon. That little knife of yours turned and twisted, but it didn't shatter. For ages I've looked for something I could wield again, and for ages I've failed to find anything. Give me a weapon, and I will reward you beyond your wildest dreams." There was a fire in his words, and I thought I was seeing the real Atal for a moment.

This man didn't want to be a king, or a ruler. No, he was a warrior. It reminded me of the old movies with the barbarian king, but this one had lost what he loved. For him, it was probably a spear or club rather than a sword, but he could no longer fight like he used to. Sure, he could tear men apart with his hands, but I imagined that it just wasn't the same.

"I'm not sure I have anything right now that would work," I admitted, not quite knowing just how strong he was.

"I do not need it right now, child. A year, ten, a hundred. I can wait; I've already waited so very long," he said.

"I'll make something," I answered carefully. "I doubt it'll work, but seeing how other weapons break might give me ideas for the future."

Finally, the old elf seemed satisfied to be done with it. The rest of the meal was eaten in silence. While I nervously thought about what I could and should make, he was staring off into the distance wistfully. Should I make him something of copper first? Steel maybe? Perhaps it would be best if I made something truly hard to break, finish this up now. There were so many things to consider, and so many projects still ongoing that I could only sigh internally.

As soon as the millennia-old monster who owned this city stopped thinking about the toy he'd soon be getting, he released me, and I rushed back home. There were a few people who looked at me oddly as I speed-walked through the streets, considering what I needed to do.

Chien was at my front door, having a staring contest with the guard left to watch my home. The guard saw me and moved out of the way, satisfied that I'd take care of things.

"Hey boss, what's up?" Chien asked as I made my way to the door.

"We have an order," I replied.

"Really? From who?"

"Atal," I announced, causing both my young assistant and the guard to freeze, their eyes growing to the size of dinner plates.

"Shit," my young protégé said, hurrying after me.

CHAPTER 9

TESTING PHASE

Atal had promised great rewards if I could make him a weapon he could wield without breaking it, but that didn't mean that I was going to hand over my best work immediately. I'd seen the man rip a woman apart with just his fists and not so much as blink; so I had to consider that he might not be that good a guy. I also wasn't quite sure what exactly he would need, and I wasn't going to be bringing out the big guns first. After all, it was better to keep some things in reserve.

I was going to start with copper, as my understanding was that he'd found a knife that had sort of worked for him. The thing about a knife was that it wasn't thick at all, so it would bend if used too harshly. To this end, a mace might actually be a better tool, or something with a longer reach. I had some things to consider.

"The most likely thing to break for him is whatever he strikes," I said to Chien as I paced. We were currently making charcoal, the first step to any extended forging, and one that was rather slow.

"Makes sense," he agreed.

"What's he likely to hit though?" I asked.

"People, big monsters, you know, whatever he wants, really. I've never met Atal; is he as amazing as they say?"

"Terrifying, but very calm, luckily for us. But absolutely terrifying," I told him.

"Mom said she saw him go after a creature once, that it was the most beautiful thing she'd ever seen." He sounded like a kid yearning for a hero as he spoke.

"I still haven't met your mom, kid. Why don't you ever bring her around?" I said. It's something that'd only come up once or twice over the years, but he'd always avoided the subject.

"She's busy," he told me. Same answer as always. It was suspicious, but the kid worked hard, so he could have his secrets.

"Anyway, club. Do you think it'll work?" I asked, since I had no clue what kind of issues we were likely to encounter.

"Maybe?"

"Other than that, something with range," I mused.

"Like a spear?"

"A spear might well work. Though, depending on how strong he is, perhaps only once. From my guess, he grips them so hard the shaft shatters, so an all-copper spear might be a good option. Then again, if he's throwing them that hard, they'd probably be destroyed in one use. Copper's not so cheap that we can use it like that yet."

I kept in mind the iron I had. I didn't have a good source of copper, so we couldn't just throw it away, but iron? Iron was everywhere, almost literally. I could get more from the shore without much effort. It would be easy to put together a bundle of iron rods for old Atal to launch like they were coming out of a fucking rail-gun. Did I want to let that out into the world yet though? I honestly wasn't sure if people were ready for it.

"So what, make rocks out of copper for him to throw?" Chien joked.

"Actually, that might not be the worst idea," I said, rubbing my chin as I thought about rock throwers.

"Same problem right? Copper not being cheap."

"Make something to throw things for him then. Make the thrower from copper and the rocks, well rocks going fast still bloody work, regardless of how fast they're going," I told him.

"They'll shatter," he answered.

"Yeah, as they slam into whatever they hit. Tomorrow we can put some mock-ups together, then we can start the casting."

"Lot of work boss," he griped.

"You want something out of this when it's all done?"

"I want a lot of things, boss, but that can all wait 'til later," he said with a grin.

"All right, grab some of the extra wood. We can at least put together some prototypes to try tomorrow."

While the charcoal burned, I made a few different variants of objects I hoped might work. Each of these would be a possible weapon for Atal, something he could try.

The first group were ball throwers, not unlike those used for dogs back on Earth. They were just a simple handle with a curve on the end. My hope was that Atal would be able to use one of these to toss rocks without having to grip them. There wasn't any reason he couldn't do that anyway, but it would be worth a shot.

The second weapon was inspired by an old video from a gentleman who liked both history and the color beige. It was a staff sling, a weapon used throughout the middle ages to hurl big rocks. This one I considered had a decent chance of failing, particularly the little rope cup that would hold the projectiles, but there was nothing to do but try. The bottom end was pointed, so we could save the effort and see how a copper spear handled his strength as well.

The next morning we headed out of the city to test the weapons in the nearby woods. I wanted plenty of room and no one watching as I tried to work out how and if these would even function. There was no objection from anyone as the two of us left with the morning gatherers, fitting right in with their ranks.

There were, however, a few odd looks. Mostly women went out to gather, and all of them had eyes on our tools. Over the last few years, I'd introduced tool after tool, and now people were starting to take a closer look at everyone who had something they'd never seen before.

As we made our way down the road out of the city, I recognized one particular girl eyeing us hard. She'd been mostly looking at Chien, but as she flicked her eyes up and met mine, I saw a flash of recognition. This was the same girl who'd been sent to spy on the sled I'd made so long ago. Based on the group she was with, though, it looked like the woman in charge of her had changed. The new head of the clique raised an eyebrow as the familiar girl rejoined them and began to whisper at speed. I didn't bother to try and hear what she was saying because when their quick conversation wrapped up, the leader approached me.

"Hello, sir. My name is Olara, and I must say, those are some interesting tools you have there," the woman said, while the others in her group followed behind her like ducklings. "Sala is one of the newest members of my group, and she said she's seen you with interesting things before. She also said you were quite kind." She gave me a light smile, her aura dancing around her lightly.

"Yes, something we're going to test," I informed her.

"Would you mind some company? I'm sure there are plenty of good places, and we did bring a bit of extra fish along today that we could share . . ." Olara asked, leaning forward slightly with a flirtatious grin.

"Normally I wouldn't mind but, unfortunately, today I do want some privacy," I informed her.

I could see Chien frowning—having cute girls flirt with you was always nice, and he was at the age where he'd be very interested in such things. If Chien were human, he'd be about fourteen now. I was pretty sure that many of the girls on the street of flowers viewed him more as a relative, or even a child, for that matter. Olara also seemed visibly disappointed, so I thought I might throw them both a bone.

"I'm busy today, but wait a cycle of the moon and come see me. I've got ideas for some digging tools that you might like, and I'm sure Chien would be more than happy to show them to you," I said, and her smile returned. "My shop is near the street of flowers. Ask a guard about Justin's place."

Shovels and spades weren't really a thing in this world yet; people dug with sticks instead. Sometimes they even found favorite digging sticks and altered them, but woodworking was laborious or needed magic, so their sticks tended to break. I could throw together a few things in moments that would make her happy, and if she used magic, like my mother, she'd be able to grow them herself later.

"You got something good for them?" Chien asked after they'd broken away from us.

"I have a couple of ideas, kid, but some free big brotherly advice first. Those girls don't like you; they like what they can get from you. It's important to know the difference and treat them accordingly." It wouldn't do for him to get head over heels for some girl who was only out to use him.

He laughed at me. "That's ironic because I don't like them either; only what I can get from them . . ."

Honestly, I didn't know if that response was good or bad, but it did make me take a longer look at the kid.

CHAPTER 10

✦

HAPPY CUSTOMER

Greetings again, youngling," Atal said as he looked over the items I'd set out.

He and his entourage had just arrived to the place I'd been directed, and I couldn't help but notice the several bound and struggling beasts pulled along after them. Going to the palace once again and asking if there was a way to get him or someone like him to test a few weapons had gotten me a very, very quick response and an open stretch of sand right near the beach.

"Greetings, Ancient. I hope the day finds you well," I replied.

Slowly, the old elf strode past the weapons laid out before him. "You think one of these might handle my strength?"

"To be honest, no. I made sure to tell the messenger it was unlikely, but without knowing where the failures might occur, I cannot make something that might succeed. This is likely to take me some time." I held myself straight, getting the feeling that he didn't want people to grovel too much without cause.

Atal didn't seem all that displeased with the answer. After all, he'd been the one to tell me that I had time. "I understand. How do these work?" he asked as he picked up the copper staff sling.

"Perhaps we should start with the club? It's the most straightforward, and will give a good measure of your power," I said, indicating the item in question.

He picked up the solid copper mace with ease, which was pretty impressive given its weight. Then he made a motion with his hand, and one of the animals was released by the guards. It was around the size of an alligator, but more in the shape of a pig. Its body was covered in stone-looking skin.

The ancient warrior blurred in my vision, one moment beside me, the next standing over the beast. His arm somehow moved even faster. The hand was simply raised one moment and down the next, accompanied by an explosive sound, and the beast's head was replaced by a crater.

One look told me nearly everything I needed to know. The shaft of the weapon had curved approximately forty-five degrees. The head of the weapon was flattened where it had struck, a complete failure of the soft metal in my book.

As he shifted it in his hands, I saw the imprint his fingers had made on the shaft. That must be why he didn't throw things; when he moved that fast his grip strength multiplied too. Maybe he'd just crushed rocks to dirt when he'd tried, each breaking under his fingers.

"That held up well," he remarked as he looked over the destroyed weapon. At my surprised look, he actually laughed before explaining. "Most things would just be bits if I used them thus. It failed, but it failed while still achieving its function."

He returned the first weapon to its place, something I was thankful for. It wouldn't ruin me if he decided to take all of these, or if they were rendered into scrap, but it did represent a high percentage of the copper currently in the city, and losing it all would be a pain. I'd already written off the staff sling/spear, which he had yet to test out.

"I see. The next two are types of throwers. Please allow me to demonstrate," I said as I picked up the one made to launch stone. Making the projectiles for this one wasn't too bad, given I'd used simple wooden balls for mine and stone for his.

I showed him how to load the weapon and then tossed the small wooden sphere down the beach a ways, getting fairly good distance. I noticed a few of his advisors perk up after seeing that.

"Interesting," he remarked as he picked up the metal version and nodded for the next beast to be released.

His first shot missed, going wide and impacting a sand dune like a meteor, but he didn't seem perturbed. Instead, he looked down at the thrower, because it had survived. Like the first weapon, I could see the indents his fingers had made, but the main body hadn't deformed much at all.

"Very interesting," he said as he loaded the next stone ball.

The poor animal was bolting as fast as it could away from a terror even greater than itself when the second ball slammed into it. I couldn't see the actual strike, but the aftereffect was clear. A cloud of gore flew upward.

My creation was now very bent though. It might survive another shot, but it probably wouldn't be accurate. But, Atal was smiling and laughing.

"Oh good, very good. You see, grandson?" he said, addressing one of the men who'd come with him. "It survived not one, but two uses, and perhaps it would even make a third. Magnificent, magnificent! Justin, you said you think you can improve these?"

It was not lost on me that he had addressed me by name, or the manic look on his face. "I . . . yes, Ancient, I think I can," I stammered under the pressure.

Then came the staff sling. My demonstration of the wooden version received even more attention from Atal's advisors. Getting the angle on its releasing notch just right had required some work, but once I did, it was just a staff with a bit of rope and a place to hold a rock. Even with it being that simple, I could still throw something the size of a baseball a couple hundred feet. Historically, the projectiles were supposed to go even further, but I was no expert.

"Ancestor, even if that doesn't work for you, we should arm some of the guard with them," one of the men spoke.

"Agreed," Atal said without even looking at him.

As I might have expected after seeing the previous two tests, this one was a total bust. Copper was just too soft, and couldn't handle the kind of stress that I was asking of it. I'd not expected the staff to break as it did, sending the top half flying, but it was unsurprising. The last of the beasts fled, with the ruler of the city seemingly unbothered by it.

"I was hoping it would survive, so you could try throwing it as well. If you look at the tip, you can see where I formed it into a spear-like shape," I commented as I frowned at the broken tool.

"I do," he remarked, turning it in his hands.

"Ah, no matter, the last one got away anyway," I said, pointing to where the small monster had turned a corner.

"Don't fret, I brought another target," he commented. "Did you think I wouldn't notice the thefts from my treasury?" he asked to nobody in particular.

One of the ministers froze, his eyes going wide. "Wait, please," he got out before the ruler turned and threw the bottom half of the staff at him.

Much like the beast that had been obliterated, the elven man's chest was torn apart. He struggled on the ground, gurgling and thrashing as the city's ruler strolled past to retrieve the projectile. I didn't find looking at the dying man easy, but I did so regardless. The spear half had been rendered into little more than scrap, malformed and just plain weird.

"Also effective, not at all bad for a first attempt, Justin. I would like you to have one of the second one remade and sent to me, then continue your work. Some people will be by tomorrow to aid you in your work as my thanks." With that, he tossed the destroyed piece lightly into the pile and turned, his people in tow.

I'd known that Atal was dangerous, but as I looked upon the corpse cooling on the beach, it reminded me just how dangerous. Either his morals were so foreign that I really just didn't understand them, or he was a psychopath—potentially both. He had an army at his beck and call, and power that I was still having trouble even properly getting a grip on.

This was something I needed to add to my to-do list, but it was something I could never speak aloud—I needed a way to stop him should it ever come to it, something to counter that old monster. Weapons would have to be made for him, but I would try to limit them where I could while I thought of something. I was going to need a weapon of unbelievable power for myself, like an orbital bombardment, or a nuke.

CHAPTER 11

DELIVERY

Getting all the scraps together from my work on Atal's prototype weapons and melting them down had been a beast of a chore. I was sad to see my work broken, but even sadder to hear that I'd be giving up more of it soon. He'd demanded I make him another ball thrower, and since I'd proved that I could, I couldn't very well deny him. At least it would be easy enough to do; it's not like I had to remake the molds or anything.

"Visitors," announced Chien as he came back from getting water.

"Yeah, Atal said he'd be sending people," I replied as I made sure my work was safe before heading to the front room.

When he'd told me he was sending people, I expected one or two to help me with materials or whatever, and perhaps another to ask questions and take notes. There were five of them in my front room, and if I was seeing correctly, another dozen in the street behind them, the latter clearly doing . . . something.

The closest to me looked to be one of the ministers from the previous day. He had a bright smile on his face as he turned to speak to me. Other than him, there was another man present from the day before, and two men who looked like guards, though they were in clearly nicer uniforms. The final one in my home irked me the most—enough that I had to struggle to keep my face neutral.

"Greetings Justin. The ancestor has sent us to see you and deliver his recompense for your hard work," the first minister said. "We've also been asked to clear out some of the houses around your home, so that you might expand."

That answered what was going on outside. "Wait, what of the people who live there?" I asked.

"Don't fret, they're being given new homes in another area," he answered, clearly understanding my hangup. "On your end, we thought you might not wish to leave."

"Thank you, what about . . ." I began.

"Ah yes, your payment," he said, motioning to someone behind them.

I recognized her instantly—the serving girl from his palace, the one I'd already turned down. She'd been covered in beads like lights on a Christmas tree, and in her hands were several bars of copper. They were small, but still enough that she seemed to struggle with the weight. The copper was something I actually cared about, seeing as it would help with making things. The girl though. Her eyes had the look of someone going to their own execution.

"The ancestor thought you might want an extra pair of hands, and he said you liked her. If she's not up to your needs, return her to the palace. I'm sure he can find one far more eager to act properly," he told me.

Yeah, Atal was definitely a psychopath. He was giving me things now to get me to hurry, and not caring about anyone else. Maybe my neighbors would get nicer homes, but I doubted it. Perhaps I could do something? Also, what about the girl? Before I could start considering it too much, the other minister stepped forward.

"While we're here, would you mind if we take a look at those weapons you used yesterday? Not the copper ones, but the wood. I've several people here who'd be very interested," he said, indicating the two guards.

"Very well, this way," I said, turning and hoping they'd all follow.

My public workshop wasn't small, but it did have the basic tools I used day-to-day, and the weapons they were interested in were still here. Everyone filed in after me and off to the side. I had the sling they were after leaned against a shelf, and I pulled it over to show to them.

"These are simple enough to make that anyone can," I explained as I passed it to one of the guards, who looked at it curiously. "The only difficult part is the notch here; see how it is angled? That's important."

Then I mimed loading and the stance needed for throwing. There was no room for that kind of thing in here, but it would give them an idea. The two guards looked at me like I was an idiot, and then at the minister.

"You're saying he used this to throw a fist-sized stone two hundred paces?" the first asked in disbelief. "And not just using his power?" It seemed he thought I'd used magic.

"Justin, would it be a bother if we borrowed this?" the minister asked nervously.

"You can have it. It's a stick and twine. I can make another with ease," I told him as I passed it over.

"And the other?" the second guard asked.

Picking that one up as well, I tossed a wooden ball into it. As I did, I put up a wall of force on the far wall and turned, using an easy motion to launch the sphere forward with some force. The two guards perked up at that. Did I need to? Not really, but I didn't want them bemoaning my products.

"This one isn't as useful since it can't really throw anything heavier than wood very well," I explained.

"We'll keep that in mind," the first of the pair said, eyeing where it'd struck.

"Now, gentlemen, while I would love to sit and talk, as you can see, my forge is going." I pointed over to the flaming construct. The smoke was leaving through a simple chimney, but it was still burning hot. "I'm sure our leader wouldn't want his new thrower delayed."

The two ministers seemed to want to talk, but the guards got the message loud and clear. Within moments, all of them were leaving my house. Chien, who'd found somewhere to hide during this whole debacle, reappeared.

"She's cute," he said, motioning to the girl who'd barely moved a muscle.

"Don't you have something better to do?" I asked.

"Not really, no." I fixed him with a glare for a few seconds before he finally smartened up. "But I can find something . . ."

"Here, I'll take these," I said to the girl, and took the copper off her hands, as Chien fled. "Do you have a name?"

"Ida," she replied.

"Well, Ida, I'm sorry for all this. I really didn't want him to send you," I began.

"Please don't send me back," she pleaded in a small voice.

"If you want to stay, you can," I assured her. "If you don't, we'll figure something out."

"Okay."

"For now, let's get some of those beads off. You know how to cook?" I desperately needed something to break the ice.

"Um . . . yes." It seemed my question had thrown her off.

"Good, cause I'm garbage at it." That wasn't really true, but I wasn't great either. "Food storage is right across the way; if you need anything, come ask. Take some time and get dinner ready, okay?" It was still morning, but I was floundering.

As she left, still looking at me like I was confusing her, I mumbled to myself. "Thanks for irritating all my neighbors and sending me a headache." Then I looked down at the pile of beads. "Least I've got funding for the next year to go along with it."

Dinner that night was awkward. Of course, Chien decided to join us just so he could laugh at the situation and, in retrospect, I was sure it would be funny from an outside perspective. I'd hid in my workshop the whole day, only once or twice having my newest . . . whatever, come to ask me where things were.

Plates were already being set up when I arrived at the table, and Ida went to take a place standing out of the way as I entered.

"No," I told her. "Make yourself one and come sit with us." She did as I told her but looked like she was waiting for the other shoe to drop the whole time. If this world had hidden camera shows, I was sure she'd be looking for them right now.

"This is great," Chien said, really amused by the whole scene. "It's like watching two toddlers trying to wrestle a fish."

"Could you not be like this?" I asked.

"No, I can't. Look at her; she's terrified, not knowing that you'd never hurt a hair on her head, and you're just completely lost. This is like the first time we met, only worse, and I'm outside of it."

"You can tell him off too, if you want," I told her before grabbing for Chien's ear, inspired by my aunt's actions when I'd been young.

". . . are you messing with me?" she finally asked. That question made my assistant break off his stream of obscenities and begin to laugh.

"No? Remember what I asked earlier about you staying or not? I meant that; if you want to leave, we'll arrange it."

"I don't have anywhere to go," she answered, seeming sad.

"If you change your mind, let me know," I told her before letting go of Chien.

"Justin, you really need to take a joke," he said, glaring at me as he rubbed his ear. "Anyway, girlie, how'd you end up all . . ." he motioned to her.

The slaves or indentured servants of this world were only kept as such for a certain number of years, shown by hash-marks on their skin. Ida was covered in them, nearly half her body. Something like that was odd, very much so, and not something I'd ever seen in the city.

"Well . . ." she began, taking a moment to sit back and organize her thoughts.

CHAPTER 12

IDA

Ida

I prepared to tell my story; one I'd already told many times. It wasn't so much that I minded, just that it was personal. Even then, I sort of wanted this Justin to know. He was a bit odd but seemed to be genuinely kind, at least so far, and I didn't want him to think badly of me.

"There's not much to it. A few decades ago, in a couple of the villages, there was a rebellion against Atal's rule," I began.

"Oh, I heard about that; didn't go too well for them," the boy, nearly a man, interrupted. I stared at him, waiting. "Sorry, continue."

"Really, there was little fighting. Our villages just refused to keep acknowledging Atal as their master. Refused his summons, refused to send him the things he told us to. The elders thought that together they could stand against him. They were wrong."

My new master, Justin, leaned back, eyes fixed on me as I spoke. He waited to hear all the details.

"I don't know how Atal would have ended up responding otherwise; not as badly as he did, perhaps, but . . . Among the envoy was one of Atal's children, his youngest. He sires them periodically—not often, but often enough. The elders killed him, sent his head back to Atal.

If only they'd known what they were doing; maybe they did and just didn't care. I don't know."

"Oh, shit," Chien remarked.

Justin continued to watch me. "What happened?" he finally asked.

"Atal came himself after that and slaughtered the elders, slaughtered the warriors they'd gathered to protect them, the hunters, the gatherers, every man, every woman. He burned the villages to the ground. Some of the children though, he spared. Not even he likes to kill the young."

"You were just a kid?" Justin asked.

"Yes, I was three. I still see it in my dreams sometimes, Atal ripping through my parents and family, then pulling apart the little tree I'd hidden in. I thought I was going to die; I was so afraid. Then he threw me to a couple of his men, told them to keep me with the others until he was done. They made me watch as he marched alone through our village. He didn't even spare those who surrendered or begged," I told Justin and his apprentice as a shiver ran down my spine.

"You're safe here. Well, as safe as I can make you," Justin assured me as he gently touched my shoulder. I really wished I could believe that.

"Thank you. Um, I'll start cleaning up if that's okay," I offered, changing the subject. We'd finished with dinner before my story had ended, and I didn't really want to keep talking. Hopefully he'd agree and let me have a few moments.

"That's fine; it's getting late anyway, and I've got to clean the workshop up too," he told me before rising. "Isn't it time for you to get going home as well, Chien?" he asked the boy.

"I suppose; see you two tomorrow. Have a good night," he said with a smirk, the jerk.

I was left alone again. In fact, I'd been left alone almost the entire day. Justin didn't seem to know what to do with me during the day, and had sent me to the residence connected to his shop. There wasn't much to it—a few workrooms I had no business in, a small cooking and eating area, a bedroom, singular; that too made my skin feel tight.

It was clear what Atal expected. He'd had me in his possession since I was a child, and he'd never tried anything with me. Once, I heard him say that he refused any woman he'd known as a child because he always saw them as kids. None of the other men around the palace had interest either, mostly because none of them were foolish enough to touch that which belonged to their master. Still, I knew the basics and what to do.

Maybe Atal was hoping that I'd produce a child for him, one who would hopefully turn out like his new favorite, Justin. As I rubbed my belly, I thought about it. Would it be so bad? At the very least, nobody would hit me for a year or two, and at best, Justin would treat me better because of it. I steeled my resolve, because I could do that, and I got the feeling that this odd man wouldn't even be bad to me.

"Need help?" I heard eventually.

"Oh, no, I'm done," I said.

"All right, I'll show you the bedroom. I've only got the one for now . . ."

I nodded. "Yeah, I saw."

He led me up the little carved stairs and into the room with the boughs built throughout it. It was nice, cozy. Justin even made a small magical light to hover near the ceiling so I could look around.

"So . . . I sleep over here, and the few times Chien's stayed, he's slept there," he said, pointing to a couple of sections of the room. "You can sleep anywhere else you want. If you need anything, let me know." With that, he turned and began to settle down.

Slowly, I moved toward him. Maybe he wanted me to approach him? As I reached out, he spoke again.

"Everything okay?"

"Y-yeah, um, no, I . . . Should I just . . ." I tried to figure out what I should do.

"Anywhere else really," he told me with a firm tone.

Carefully, I went over to one of the empty segments of boughs and sat down, looking over at him. He was going to sleep, to *sleep*? Was he all right? Did he not like me? I'd seen him looking at me at Atal's palace. Maybe he didn't like women? Really, I didn't know.

The light faded long before my questions did. Those nagging worries kept me up well into the night.

The next morning when young Chien saw me, he began to laugh uproariously. He even took time to point at my face like he knew this was going to happen. I'd already decided that I couldn't stand him, but this was a bit much.

"You knew what would happen," I accused.

"Your face is amazing," he said between bouts.

"Does he like guys?" I asked.

"Oh decidedly not," the boy answered.

"Then why is he—"

"Sweetheart, I've known him for years, and I still don't get it. If you start to understand why he is the way he is, you let me know."

Over the next few weeks, I discovered that Chien was right. Justin seemed to have some kind of moral code, but I didn't understand the reasoning behind it, and he didn't seem to want to explain too deeply. He didn't care about a lot of the things people really cared about here, and did care about things most people ignored. One day he got very excited about something, but when I inquired about it, his explanation made no sense.

Then there were the tasks I was sometimes given. He had me doing a lot of things with fur and plant fiber—making very thin ropes, almost too thin to even hold together. Then I had to do all these other things with them like looping and doing a weird column and row thing. It was easy but tedious. He told me his fingers were too big and clumsy, and using his power to do it was a pain, so it was now my job.

In the end though, my new master was nice. He didn't treat me like I was his possession, but as a person, making sure I had plenty of food and nice clothes and somewhere safe and warm to sleep. There were even some beads set aside for me to buy the things I wanted. Altogether, this was a pretty good life; odd, but good.

CHAPTER 13

✧

MAGICAL MATERIALS

Ida was working out wonderfully. I'd put her on the fabric project I'd given up on a couple of years ago. The work was outside of my wheelhouse. Perhaps she'd have better luck with it, and if nothing else, I might get a bit more material to work with from her. My own attempts had been successful, in a certain light. I'd managed to make some rough cloth, but wildly failed because of the sheer amount of mana I'd had to waste doing it. Spinning was hard, and no matter what I tried, I just couldn't get my fingers to make it work.

Having Atal as a backer did have some other benefits though. I'd sent a messenger to the palace to ask about magical materials recently, and I'd been told that I could come by later today to talk to some people. That was exciting, as I'd had little success working with those materials as of yet. Even if I couldn't find something for Atal's project, perhaps I could find something for my own. C

It was still early though, so I was taking some time to get work done in my underground lab. A small portion of my copper had been converted into wire, and I was in the process of building a proper computer. Games here I came! Ha! More like basic math, poorly and with some bugs, but one thing built upon another, and with time I could build high.

I'd not yet discovered anything approaching a proper medium for magic, nor was I worrying about it at the moment. Instead, this was good ol' electricity, and honestly, poorly made. One day I might have access to pure silicon crystals and the ability to inscribe upon them advanced patterns. I could even see what that would look like in my mind, but I lacked the know-how and the architectural mind for it.

The memory that came with being an elf had given me one advantage that I'd never dreamed of as a man. My perfect memory; it was so much, so amazing. Even now, I could remember everything down to the tiniest fragment. This meant that if I could ever figure out how a computer worked, or a chip, I could make them. Once I'd committed the design to memory, I could probably build it atom by atom with my magic. It was amazing, unbelievably powerful, and something I'd do eventually. I promised myself that.

For now though, I began working my way through exponents, looking for obvious issues with my current labor. It was rough, very rough, and I had to power it manually—put in the digits manually and everything else manually—but it could tell me what two to the power of twelve was, so that was something. Eventually, I would need to make some kind of proper programs to go into these, not something I cherished doing. I'd been a garbage programmer in my last life, only ever knowing the basics. I'd always been much more of a hardware guy.

A few more hours of playing around and it was time to leave. There weren't any clocks around here, more like general times of day, but being on time was polite. My work wasn't going anywhere for now. So, with a few flicks of my wrist I locked up my workroom and headed out.

Before I left, I went to check on my workers. Chien was sharing a few different shovel designs with a group of girls who were paying very close attention to his movements. I wasn't sure exactly which would work best for them, so I'd armed him with a few made of wood, from small gardening trowels to larger digging implements. None of these would be all that hard for them to make, but the shift in thinking was what we needed. Ida was in her little work area and looked up at me as I came in the door.

"Oh, hello, um, Justin," she said, still awkward around me.

"Good morning, Ida," I replied. "How are things going?"

"Oh, very well. So, you know how you told me to brush out the fibers before using them?" she asked.

"Yes."

"Well, if you do that and make sure they're all in the same direction, you can roll them up, and . . ." She began to demonstrate how she'd changed the direction of the fiber she was using. I could also see she'd spent a lot more time separating them and combing them before bothering with this. It was the end result that I was interested in though.

"Your thread," I said, pointing to the little spool there. "May I?" I could've just taken it, but being nice and respectful was important.

After quick confirmation, I unspooled a bit. She'd managed to outdo me on this, and while it certainly wouldn't match the fine silk stuff Earth had, it was more than good enough to make cloth from. It was thin, and quite regular.

"Excellent work," I said, giving her a smile and patting her on the shoulder. She turned, but I didn't miss the slight blush that crept up her face. "Now, I must be off."

She waved me off, as did Chien when he saw me leaving. The trip to the palace was quite a walk, but not too bad. When I got there I saw something I'd not expected—they were renovating. The entrance was getting an arch put over it, something which raised my eyebrows quite high.

Rather than being taken to Atal, I was taken off to a side room, where I was greeted by a woman who instantly set my hair standing on end. She was a full head shorter than I was, but half of her hair was white, and her expression spoke of stark disapproval.

"Good day, miss . . ."

"Jina, you may call me Jina. Before we start, I will inform you that I disapprove of this heavily." She had a strong frown as she spoke.

"What about, if I may ask?"

"You may. You're too young for this Justin, far too young. Normally, even the simplest of these secrets wouldn't be given to someone until they had their first white hair, but Grandfather has spoken highly of you and insisted himself. Let me inform you though that some of what I will be showing you is banned, and for good reason. If it is misused, you will die, either at your own hands or Atal's. Am I understood?"

"Yes, clearly understood," I answered.

"Good, follow me." With that, Jina turned and began walking away.

As she showed me to her room, the only conclusion that I could reasonably come to was that she was the closest thing to an honest-to-goodness witch I'd seen since coming to this world. It looked like a bright and airy workspace, with hanging herbs, mushrooms, and even a few rocks in piles and atop simple shelves. Some were even in bowls of various types. A few glowed with eerie light, and a few had auras. In one corner, there was a beast in a wooden cage, where the tree had been grown around it to keep it in place. The beast let out angry hisses and odd squeaking noises.

"Sit," I was told, a finger pointing to a spot near a little table. As soon as I'd found my place, Jina began pacing, now able to tower over and look down at me. "I will be showing you general recipes for a number of potions and dyes today, along with some other, less common, materials. If ingested, the first of these will raise your power significantly, but at the same time, cause your death. The magic in it spreads and burns through you, and once the process begins, it cannot be ended."

". . . I've seen something like that before," I told her.

"Oh? And what happened to the drinker?" she said with genuine curiosity.

"He . . . he went mad, and I had to kill him." I couldn't look up as I spoke, the memory still fresh.

"Not unusual, and I'm glad you've seen it, so you know the dangers."

As she explained each herb, she took it down, listing uses, where to find it, what it was called by some people, and others that might be used in its place. Some needed to be dried, or crushed, or wet. I watched as she prepared almost a dozen of the brews that I knew were fatal. Each time, she would tell me who'd made them, how they'd died, and the destruction they'd caused. It was going to be a long afternoon.

CHAPTER 14

CONDUCTOR

Jina had the bedside manner of a bag of angry bees, and her poor victim, who'd come in to get a tattoo, was in incredible pain and crying by the time she left. I felt bad for the girl.

"You could have numbed her," I pointed out after Sina made her way out the door.

"I could have," Jina agreed. "But, as it stands, she learned a valuable lesson, and I think you might have too."

"And what would that be? Not to piss you off?" I guessed.

"Not to irritate those more powerful than you. You need to remember that, because I am far more forgiving than my grandfather, though admittedly, easier to anger."

I looked at the tool she'd been using. This wasn't the modern world, and they didn't have something like a tattoo gun; instead it was simpler, and not in a good way. There was also magic involved though; I'd seen that much. Jina had something going on as she moved along, something that got the ink locked in faster, and I doubted it would leak or fade much with time. Sadly, that sort of thing wasn't my wheelhouse.

"Why tell me that though? To scare me? I've already seen Atal in action, and I assure you I've no desire to anger him, or you, for that matter. It seems that neither of you would have a problem killing me if I did anything to warrant it. Or is it that your grandfather wants this done, and done right?"

"The latter, and something for you to understand for later. If he's calling upon you now, others will in the future. Keep that in mind while you consider what you do," she replied with a sigh at the end. Perhaps she didn't hate me, if she was trying to get me to learn this without hurting me. Then again.

"I'll keep it in mind."

"Good, any questions on the other materials we've covered here? If so, please ask them now."

For a moment or two, I moved around the room, checking to make sure I'd not missed anything. Ingredient by ingredient I looked, one after another, to make sure I'd followed her lessons. None of these seemed useful in the least, well not to me anyway. I was frowning until I came upon a small crystal that I'd not seen before. It was elongated and had not been carved in any way I could see.

"What's this do?" I asked, pointing. There were things in this room I wasn't willing to touch.

"Oh, that's just a curiosity. If enough power goes through a small enough space, it sometimes forms those. Grandfather gave me that one; it came out of a beast of some kind." She seemed to disregard it.

"Does it do anything?" I asked.

"Not anything useful. All it does is move a small amount of its energy from one side to another."

At my blank look she rolled her eyes and came over to me. "Watch."

My teacher picked up the stone and began focusing. I could see her aura focus around her finger, which she then poked to one side of the stone. What I saw next was difficult to describe, as it happened in both magical sight and a physical one. The mana traveled through the stone along a path that branched and came back together, like those weird shapes lightning made. Where it met at the end, a small amount of aura and light poured out, barely enough to see, but it was there.

"Do they break easily?" I asked, my eyes never leaving her demonstration; it was perfect.

"No, but like I said, they're pretty hard to find. This one came out of a truly massive beast. It had a horn that shot out beams of burning light. You'll not be able to find a source around here or anywhere else." I could sense her frowning at me, even though I didn't look. "They don't work in any potion or tattoo either. I've tried."

It was the conductor I'd been looking for, and it might, just might, have an output as well. It was perfect, completely perfect. How to make one though. How to create such a thing. She'd said these stones could only be found in places where a lot of magic had been concentrated in a very small area, and perhaps that was the answer. I didn't know yet, but I knew that I needed to find out.

"I need to look into this," I said quietly.

"You can't have it; this one is mine." There was a tinge of childish greed in her tone that made me blink. When I looked up at Jina, she was frowning.

"Um, I meant the item in general, not this specific one. If others are found though, I'd like to see them," I said, trying to waylay any issue.

"Ah, I see. If any others are found I'll keep that in mind, but they don't turn up often at all." Her hands were tight around the little stone, and I wondered if there was more that I'd missed. She'd said it was a gift, so maybe she had a sentimental attachment to it.

After a few more awkward minutes, I left and was quite tired, but with a new idea that might one day lead me to greatness. Perhaps not today, but one day, I could see that stone and what it did becoming something more.

Unfortunately, I was waylaid on my way out by one of the king's advisors I'd met just a few days prior. He'd not shared his name, and I'd not cared, but he smiled when he saw me.

"Hello again," he said. "I was hoping you'd come up with some new weapons. Everyone loves those stone throwers, but they're limited."

"Sorry, not at the moment. Was there some important need for them in particular?"

There was a look on his face as he formed his words that was hard to describe. "Yes and no. Nothing at the moment, but whispers from the west. I'm sending some of the guards out to look around, to make sure things are well. That said, I don't think we'll have any problems."

"Are you looking for something to use for close combat or long range?" I asked. Weapons really weren't what I knew much about, but if he had some idea of what he wanted, maybe I could come up with something. Then again, there were only so many ways to cut, stab, or bludgeon someone to death.

"Close," he answered.

"Right, I'll think about it, see if anything comes to mind." Honestly I was far more interested in trying to make magic crystals though.

CHAPTER 15

CRIMSON

I had a lead, but a lead was not an answer. That crystal was the thing I needed, just the thing, and if I could get it right and make it work like I wanted it to . . . well, the possibilities were nearly endless, weren't they?

Before I could go forward with that plan, though, I had a number of problems. These crystals were formed by large quantities of magic in tiny spaces, but how large? How small a space? How did I get them to do what I wanted, or form where I wanted? Did I even have enough magic to make it happen on my own?

Time would answer these questions, time and research. My days fell into my downstairs lab, trying to get the answers, refusing to leave my questions unanswered. I had my lead, and I was going to chase it down until I found what I needed to truly bring this world to the next level.

Successes were . . . slow. The first thing I needed to do was recreate even that small example I'd seen. This proved difficult, as I guessed it might. Magic, it turned out, did not want to be shoved into a space that small.

I leaned over my workspace, pushing against an imaginary point, trying to shove my light spell into it. This was proving not only difficult but dangerous. So much energy focused in one location wasn't something to be scoffed at. I was even running some calculations to see just how dangerous this would be.

My first attempt at making a light crystal had me blinking until I could see again. One trip to a local healer to fix the dark spot in my vision later, and I was back at it, this time with more shielding. A few attempts in, and I decided that glass wouldn't be enough. On second thought, this would all need to be done in an iron box.

Again and again I tried, and again and again I failed. There was something I was missing. The small cube, about a centimeter across, that I was trying to make just wouldn't form, no matter what I tried. Was I going for an area too large? That seemed ludicrous, but perhaps it was true. Maybe it had something to do with the light itself.

Jina had described the creature as projecting dangerous beams of light. What was dangerous though? Dangerous to me? I was pretty sure I'd already managed that. Dangerous to Atal? More difficult, but if he'd stood in the light I was making, I doubted he'd enjoy it. Was there something in that line of thinking?

It struck me. The light that I was trying to make was just that, generally light. Maybe if I focused on one particular wavelength, I'd have better success. It had already been weeks, so a few hours of playing with magic until I could get just one wavelength wasn't too bad. I settled on red, figuring it would have the least energy.

That night I slept in my lab, aiming to start first thing in the morning. Having to go through the motions of dealing with Chien and Ida when I was like this would be too much, so I didn't. I cared for them, certainly, but for the moment, I wanted this done, and done right.

How long had I been down here, I wondered, not thinking too deeply. I'd tried to go back up every day, tried to see my friends at least briefly between spats of work, but they had been pretty short visits. After this, I would need to take a break, a longer one, and maybe go out into the city for a day and clear my head.

Before that, though, I extended my hands, using my magic to imagine the perfect spot within the container. Right in the center, I formed the cube and began the process of making a light within it. Little by little, I forced the magic in; more, then more, as much as I could. I kept pushing, kept trying to make the light even brighter.

The box began to radiate heat, but I didn't let that stop me, didn't let my focus waver. Bit by bit, I pushed, the magic struggling and rebelling against me, trying to refuse to be manipulated any further. That wouldn't do, so I kept on, more and more, as hard as I could.

A red glow began to shine from the box, not from the light leaking through, but from the heat. I'd reached this point before. Beads of sweat flowed down my face as both the heat and the effort took its toll, yet nothing felt different yet.

Even as I struggled, disbelief began to dawn on me. There had to be a limit, a point at which even the laws of physics would rebel. This much energy all in one space, all in one point, wasn't supposed to be. Could I make a nuke if I wanted to? I'd not really tried, but this much power in one spot wasn't unlike that kind of reaction. Not quite there, but getting close.

In desperation to see this done, I mentally grabbed the sides of my box of light magic and began to push, smaller and smaller. It resisted, the energy trying to refuse my efforts, trying to keep itself in a larger space, but I would have none of it.

My power was nearly spent, the mana used to fuel my magic flowing into this construct like water down a drain, faster and faster as I tried to push it to a new limit. With a roar of anger at my failures, I heaved all I could into the spell, smashing the little construct of light into as tiny of an area as I could make it.

The box I was using to contain this magic glowed bright yellow, nearly white, as I slammed the last of my magic into it. Oppressive heat poured off it and into the room, enough to make my hands hurt and the smell of scorched hair drift to my nostrils. But as the last of my mana moved, there was a tiny *pop* in my senses as the spell reacted to it and the magic disappeared all at once.

Barely a second passed before my knees buckled. I was out of mana, and my body rebelled, head swimming as I emptied my stomach onto the floor of my lab and passed out. Perhaps I'd pushed just a bit too hard.

I wasn't sure how long I'd lain there, unconscious, but it had to have been hours. When I woke up, I had a raging headache and felt like I'd lain out in the sun asleep for a day, the light burning my skin. That said, I was alive, and even if my head pounded, and the idea of standing made me want to puke, I thought I'd succeeded.

The iron box was still hot, so after taking a moment to drink some water and rub my temples, I carefully floated it away. Even that expenditure of magic was a bit much, though, my body still weak after how much I'd done.

Eagerly, I looked for my prize, but no crystal sat there. Jina's had been a couple of inches across, and I was aiming for one smaller, but nothing—no crystal, no rock, nothing. I looked in the top of the box. Nothing. Again I looked at the table, hoping to find at least a small nugget, but there was nothing.

I'd felt something form, something pop in there. Where was it? Had the heat destroyed my prize? Had I made a mistake? I didn't know.

For almost a minute, I sat and cursed, looking at the blank table. Then I had an idea.

Turning out all the lights, I turned once more to the little stone table I'd used, and I began to form a new spell. I pushed out my magic, just pure magic, in a light mist. I went slowly, so slowly, trying to see if I could find the missing stone.

It was subtle at first, but moments later, there was a soft red light. It was the same red my spell had been making, the same ruby tone that I was trying to form. The point was small, so small, and with care I licked the tip of my finger and touched it to the spot where the red speck was located.

There, stuck to the tip of my pointer finger was my crystal, and no wonder I'd missed it. It was only the size of a grain of sand. The light it gave off wasn't much—just enough to notice—but it was beautiful. It also led me to a new question.

"How much magic did that fucking monster have?!" I screamed into the darkness, careful not to lose my prize.

I had to wait a while to recharge fully, but as I did, I built a diamond around the little grain. I'd used these several times already for my experiments and I didn't want to lose this power source. A small laugh escaped my lips as I realized that making what was considered one of the premium stones back on Earth was now child's play to me in comparison.

For a long time I sat there with my new little toy, feeding it wisps of mana and basking in the soft glow it radiated in return. All things had to come to an end though. A small bell eventually began to chime, a message from Chien that I was needed upstairs.

Putting my new plaything down, I headed up the little staircase and out into the main workshop. My assistant looked at me with blinking eyes, seemingly alarmed.

"Uh, boss, you okay? You look like shit," he said. "Ugh, you also smell like shit."

"Long day. What do you need?" I said curtly; though admittedly, I did need a bath.

"There's these two women here, refuse to leave until they speak to you," he told me. "Though if you go out smelling like that, I'm sure they will."

"Why?" I asked.

"Said they're looking for a coppersmith, hoped you might know the guy."

"Fine, fine, I'll go see them."

I quickly marched through the house. It was a pain to be interrupted when I was working, and with a new breakthrough, these two needed to go. There was research to be done, and no need for me to be out here talking to random people.

As the door opened I saw them. Atie was there, a long scar running across her face, healed, but not old. Beside her was Isha, who looked to have grown inches since last we'd met. My aunt and my closest friend from my village were here, but something was off. Their eyes . . . they looked tired and . . . sad?

"Elian!" my aunt called when she saw me, rushing forward to wrap her arms around me. "You're all right, and you're here!"

"Hey, Auntie," I said, shocked. It was quite surreal seeing them in my house.

"And you smell! What in the world?" she asked, looking me over. "Is that vomit?"

"You're not looking so great yourself. Why didn't you get mom to heal that?" I asked, poking her scar.

Instantly I saw her shoulders fall. She turned to Isha, refusing to meet my eyes. In that moment I felt my heart stop, seeming to have been ripped from my chest.

CHAPTER 16

END OF ELAYATOL

Isha

I lay back, thinking of what was soon to come. As the years had passed, I'd kept an eye on Elian's mother, waiting for the day when she would split from our tribe, when I could see my friend once more. Soon, it would be soon; already there were white hairs starting to form on her crown—just a few, but enough for her to split. Any day now she'd make that call, and I couldn't wait to see Elaya's face when she did.

Ever since the fire and the banishments, the village had been split, the rift growing deeper almost by the day. The elder's closest people kept close to her, always near, but they were few and weak compared to those gathering around Adia. So much so that the older woman might be pressured to leave. We also had nearly every user of fire in Adia's circle, which was another powerful motivator.

"Time for the split is near," Atie said as she slid in beside me. "Have you thought about our offer?"

"To leave my family's hut and come join yours?" I asked, smiling at her.

"It's a good option, and when we get Elian back it will put you in the right position . . ."

"You're assuming he hasn't found someone else," I retorted. "And what about his parents? They're accepting of this? My family wasn't exactly well off before I came along, and they're not particularly thrilled with how I'm aligning either."

"Accepting? Sweetling, Eduan's the one who suggested it, said his son would need someone to help keep him in line," the older woman answered. "Though I wouldn't wish that job on anyone," she added with a snicker.

It was a good offer, to move from where I was to join them. It would also cement my position more than anything else. Already I was moving more in the circle that Elian's mother led, gathering more with them, trading more with them. The few girls my age who'd fallen in with me were reaping benefits from our association.

Sadly, my parents didn't approve at all. Mother, particularly, didn't like Elian after the fire; though, I sensed she'd been holding a grudge for some time. She was trying to get me to side with Elaya in the coming conflict, as she seemed to believe it the safer option. It likely had to do with the fact that if Elaya and I were the only ones with power left in the village, our standing would climb through the trees.

"Let's talk later," I finally answered, not wanting my decision to be overheard.

"Sounds good to me," Atie answered in a singsong voice.

That evening as everyone headed back to the village, the two of us broke off. There was a small overlook atop a rock on the path. It was visible just in case something happened, but private enough for us to speak without being bothered. I'd have preferred to speak to Adia myself, but that would have been too obvious, too forward. As we settled in, I looked at Atie, trying my best to harden my face.

"If I do this, it means I'll be basically alone, dependent on your family. Should that happen and you betray me, I'll never forgive you," I said.

"Nor would my nephew. You know what he's like, and you know how he feels about you. We really do want you with us," she said. Her voice was calm, if a bit chiding, but overall sincere.

"Okay then, since nobody's going out tomorrow, I'll do it then. I want to make this transition during the day when my parents won't have the time to corner me beforehand. What about some of the others who run with my gathering group?"

"You'll have to speak with them, see where they fall," Atie replied with a shrug. "Obviously we do want more people, but if they don't want to, then it's no major issue."

"Okay, I'll do that—" I was interrupted by angry yelling, and I turned to the village. "What?"

A group had come from the far side of the woods and met with the returning men. These people were dressed differently, and many of them were armed. They all seemed to be male, except the one in front, a girl. She was slightly familiar. Their arrival had set off a ruckus, and instantly people were yelling. The men, led by Larus, moved to the front.

"Is that Cala?" Atie asked, squinting at the converging masses of people. "This isn't good."

Elaya had moved to stand beside Larus, hands igniting with some form of power. I didn't know what she'd do, but the conditions of any exile were strict—if you returned, you died. Before the elder could act, though, another strode from the trees. A man with hair of pure white walked toward the confrontation like the world was his. Cala's arm linked through his as he moved beside her.

"Atie . . ." I said.

"Very not good."

From our vantage point, I couldn't hear the words that were being exchanged, but the results were instant. Before anyone could act, there was a noise like a thousand rolls of thunder, and everyone standing before the interlopers ceased to be. One second they were there, then they weren't, replaced by a wall of destruction, the likes of which I'd never seen. Wood was splintered, the ground was torn apart, the people were reduced to little more than chunks of red.

For an instant I froze, the whole world froze, and there was perfect silence and stillness. No birds or insects chirped, and even the wind seemed to briefly die. Then the screaming began as the surviving villagers tried to flee, but the newcomers fell upon them like wolves.

I almost jumped as a hand wrapped around my wrist, pulling me hard.

"We need to run!" Atie nearly screamed, pulling me as she turned.

Before we could move, there was a flash of movement. My companion fell as the man who'd snuck up behind us slashed out with a black stone knife, drawing a line of red across her face. Had we not been turning to flee, he'd have likely killed her.

"I'm sorry, girls," the strangely dressed man said. "Can't have any witnesses."

He'd misjudged, and I screamed. Those like me had few attacks we could use, but I'd been taught this one. I could scream loudly enough to disorient, to harm. For a moment, I realized that this was the same attack that had just been used on the village, but that wasn't important right now. What was important was the result of my own at this moment.

Our attacker fell, dropping his weapon. Without missing a beat, Atie scooped it up and plunged it handle-deep into his chest, causing him to gasp and thrash, breath sounding wet as he struggled to take in air.

"Your face," I said to her.

"No, run," she answered, retaking my hand and pulling me away into the forest.

We ran as night fell, taking the world into shadows. On we ran, using the stars as our guide, eastward, ever eastward and toward the coast, away from whoever these men were, and whatever they wanted. After a time we stopped for a break, giving me a chance to patch up Atie's face and to plan.

There wasn't much to plan though. The village was gone. The other villages we knew of were too close to it, too near to be spared if those monsters wished to take them. Only one place might be safe. Elian had fled to the city of Atal, and its ruler was said to be mighty. If his parents survived, certainly they'd go there too, to collect their son. That might be the only way to reconnect with whatever family and friends were left.

CHAPTER 17

✦

WEAPONS FOR A MONSTER

As Atie and Isha recounted the events that took place in Elayatol, I stood up. I was numb, cold. How many of the people I knew were dead? My parents? Probably, Larus? Ninden? I didn't know if they were gone or not. Perhaps some would find me, perhaps not.

"Ida, show these two where they can sleep, please. I have work to do."

"Wait, hold on," Atie said, stepping in front of me. "You look and smell like death. You need to wash and sleep; then we can talk about whatever you plan to do."

"What I plan to do is deliver to Atal what he desires and hope that he can slaughter those bastards," I answered, dripping cold fury, "because I'm still not powerful enough to do it myself."

"Wash, sleep," she commanded, not moving an inch.

I could have moved her, could have made her do what I wanted. I very nearly did, until a small hand touched my arm.

"Elian, please," Isha said, looking worried.

"Fine, you're right. I need to be fresh for what comes next. You two need to make sure someone here in Atal knows what happened. Chien, can you help them with reporting the attack on Elayatol?" I asked.

"I got it, boss," he said, looking at me with concern.

"Good, if you need me, you know where I'll be."

"Never seen him that mad before," I heard the boy say as I left the room. "And I wouldn't want to be on the receiving end of it."

I could make water, but I wasn't particularly good at it, and using a hot stream to wash myself clean only took a few minutes. Afterward, I returned to my room and fell into bed. It took time to calm my mind, for though physically I was spent, my mind was racing. No matter what I tried, I couldn't rest my mind, so I just lay there, staring at the ceiling.

After an hour I was still awake, still unable to get even a wink of rest, tossing and turning. Around that time Isha appeared. She didn't say anything, didn't speak, or ask how I was. Instead she lay down beside me and curled up.

"What are you doing?" I asked.

"I need somewhere I can feel safe. Without that, I'm not sure I'll sleep at all," she answered without opening her eyes.

"And you came here?" I said in disbelief.

"Of course. I know you're safe to be around. Now let me sleep."

For a moment I wanted to throw her out and make her go elsewhere, but I couldn't bring myself to do it. Nor could I, in good conscience, disturb her. So I tried to stay still, tried to let her sleep, if she could. Then at least one of us would. After a few minutes I found that stilling my body stilled my mind, and the faint rhythm of her breathing calmed me. I didn't know exactly how long it took, but shortly thereafter I too found rest.

When I returned to the waking world it was dark, and quiet. My rage wasn't gone, but it was hardened like steel. No longer did I burn, but now I felt like a blade, sharper, more ready. I slipped away into my shop, and there I began the process of forging.

Iron and steel weren't like copper. Copper you mostly cast, only forging the edges, but not iron. No, iron had to be forged, beaten, and pounded into shape. I wasn't particularly good at it, but with magic to help me, I could go fast, and so I did.

I took a steel billet, a shaft of deadly metal for those who'd done so much wrong, and carved a point on one edge and did the same with another beam. These would function more like rods from a rail-gun than anything else, but having blades on the ends of them might help. I didn't know for sure.

Once the desired shape was achieved, I let them set. Steel could be a finicky thing, the internal stresses dangerous. The solution was simple—heat it well and then let it sit, either out in the open or in ashes. This fixed the stress, allowing the piece to survive better.

With magic, I could work faster than anything or anyone, short of a machine, and soon had half a dozen of the spears resting. In the afternoon, I would begin working on them again. I didn't know how long that would take, but the time would be well spent.

Then I worked on the thrower, much like the one I'd already made for the ancient warrior. Getting it to the right shape was weird, the metal moving like clay as I worked it into shape. Once I was happy with it, I put it to the side as well, sure that it would be even more breakable than the spears, but in a very different way.

For ammo, well, rocks would probably do. I considered making them of iron as well but worried that the added weight would destroy the thrower even faster. It shouldn't matter much that they weren't as hard. At the speed Atal moved, even a stone would be deadly.

Several of the bells in my shop rang. Wondering what the issue was now, I went upstairs. There I found the women in my house involved in a glaring competition, food laid on my little table in a spread.

"What do you need?" I asked the three women.

"I know you don't like being disturbed, but they were insistent," Ida said first, indicating the other two.

"You need to eat, nephew," Auntie Atie said. "Regardless of what she thinks."

Isha nodded in agreement.

"Fine," I answered. "I was at a good enough stopping point anyway. Did you report the attack?"

"An elder by the name of Shorin came by to speak with us. He asked after you, but we knew you were busy, so . . ." Isha said.

"Good, Shorin's an ally of sorts," I said with a pleased nod. If they were sending him out, it meant this was being taken seriously. "I'll make my delivery to Atal tomorrow, perhaps speak with him then."

"Are you really on speaking terms with him?" Auntie Atie asked as I took my first bite.

"Yes," I answered shortly. "He likes my weapons. Sent me a bunch of beads as a thank you, and he sent me Ida over there to help."

"Did he now?" Isha said, giving the other girl a narrow-eyed look.

"Indeed, which I didn't ask for. If I send her back to him though, he's not likely to take kindly to that, so I'm letting her stay and help. She sleeps in the room down here." I hoped that the last part would clear up any misconceptions about the relationship between me and Ida. I liked Isha and didn't want her jealous of a girl I'd never actually been with.

"I see," she said, seemingly not totally convinced, but mollified.

"Now if you'll excuse me, I've work to return to." In the time it had taken to speak, I'd finished everything on my plate. "Thank you for the food."

Once I was certain that my steel had cooled, I hardened the spear tips. The thrower didn't need hardening, but I'd found that with points and blades, it helped. Rather than water or oil—or something insane like the urine of a redheaded virgin or blood—I found that a mixture of extremely soapy water and salt worked best. It was a strange concoction, and the points sounded like they were screaming as they cooled in the mix, but they came out harder than I could have hoped.

Someday, I would figure out how to integrate magic for this process, but for now, something deadly was needed, and that is exactly what I had now.

CHAPTER 18

✦

MEETING

It would have been a struggle to get everything to Atal's palace, but I had magic, so lifting things wasn't a problem. As I picked my way through the streets, people gave me odd looks when they saw the bundle of floating spears and the tool tied to my back. But it wasn't the oddest thing that had ever happened in Atal, so they let me be.

Though, as I came to the palace gates where the guards were standing, it occurred to me that it might just be that I was being followed by well over a hundred pounds of metal that had them wide-eyed, not that it was floating. There was a zero percent chance that someone wouldn't come looking for the new material, but at this point, I didn't really care. They didn't know how to make it, and I wasn't going to share just yet, not until this war was settled.

"I've a delivery for Atal," I told the guard.

"You're Justin, right? Bring it in." The man waved me through and had a servant show me to a side room. Having called ahead really helped.

"Should I just leave these?" I asked the man.

"I believe the ancient will wish to speak with you. He told us that should you bring him something, we should notify him immediately. So, would you please wait here?" the servant asked nervously. I supposed he was in a similar boat as Ida, based on his markings, and he had requested I wait, not ordered.

"Certainly, I'd like to speak to him as well," I answered, trying to keep the stress from my voice.

Soon enough Atal appeared, a smile on his face as he nearly bounced into the room.

"Ah, Justin, or should I say Elian? Regardless, welcome. What do you have for me?" he enthused as he moved over to the spears and the stone chucker. This was concerning. He must have heard about Isha's and Atie's report. Who knew how he'd react.

"Same design as before, though this material should be significantly more durable. I doubt it can fully stand up to your strength, but this metal is far more common than copper, though harder to work with," I said as he moved to pick up one of the spears.

Atal lifted what was effectively a solid rod of iron as if it were made of wood, turning it around in his hands. These movements got faster and faster, though he did at times stop to examine how it was holding up. It didn't take long for a smile to form on his face, blooming bigger and bigger as he played with his new toy.

"I'll need to test these, but they do seem better." On a whim, he reached forward and bent one of the spears, which was saying something as they were almost an inch thick of steel. "Probably not quite there, but excellent progress. I was hoping that you might have worked magic into them, though, but you have not?"

"I was trying to but have come to an impasse with the crystals," I answered with a frown.

"Yes, my granddaughter told me that you were quite interested in the one I gave her when she was little. Jina is a dear, isn't she? Used to be so terrified of the darkness that the crystal seemed to be the only thing to help. Shame that they're so rare."

I nearly laughed as it struck me that the rare material that I'd wanted so badly had actually been that cruel woman's childhood nightlight. That did explain her reaction to my desire for it. A gift your grandpa had given you when you were a kid to bring you comfort was a rare thing.

"And difficult to make," I agreed, nodding.

That was apparently not an expected answer, as his head snapped toward me. "You made one?" he asked with slightly widened eyes.

"Not like hers. It's small, about the size of a grain of sand, and making it took everything I had. I think that in the future, they may be a basis for greater weapons yet, but after finishing it, I realized that any attempt at making a weapon that advanced will take a very long time." He might want more from me now, but that was a risk I could take, because I needed his attention too.

"That is something I would like to see, but I get the feeling you have something else?" Atal asked with slightly more seriousness.

"Yes, you've heard about the attack on Elayatol, haven't you?"

"I have, a worrying report. I don't mind you lying about your name; though, I don't understand it. If that's what you're worried about?" he said with a shake of his head.

"Didn't think you would, though appreciated. No, I'm worried about the village in general. How will you respond?" This was a real worry of mine; if he let it go, then I'd have to figure out how to kill this other ancient as well.

"I haven't decided," Atal replied. "There will need to be retribution, of course, but attacking such a remote village is odd. Honestly, I'm not sure why he bothered. Not like there's anything there."

"Do you know the full story of why I was banished from my village?" I asked.

"No."

I proceeded to tell him everything about Rindal, about Cala, about the kids. As I went on, the slightly jovial boy who wanted a new weapon to play with disappeared. Before me once more sat a ruler, eyes sharp and ears tuned in to what I was saying. He didn't interrupt, letting me go until I was finished.

"Since Cala was with them, I suspect they may be after the pool," I explained.

"Indeed. You may not know this since you've never gathered them, but those potions use rare ingredients. Using them on, for instance, an army has never been possible, but with that much . . ." His eyes drifted away as he thought. "You said these were made from a common material," he said, indicating the one he held. "How common?"

"It will take time to make them, but I can make as many of those spears as you want." It was an easy truth.

"Good, because I suspect I will need more, and more for my best warriors. Justin, do you prefer Justin?" he asked.

"I do." I nodded.

"Justin, make spears as you can, and if you can improve them, excellent. I'll buy them all at whatever price you find fair. Thank you for bringing this to my attention."

With a conflicted face, I spoke. "I'll freely admit to it serving my own wants, Ancient. They likely killed my family, and I'd like to see them dead."

"True, but if you speak the truth about that pool, it must be secured. I notice you didn't seem to object to your banishment?"

"No, in the end I did cause quite a lot of damage, didn't I? I didn't like it, but I understood." I could only shrug, since Elaya did have a point. You couldn't have people known for starting forest fires in a village surrounded by trees.

"With Elaya's death, it will be over; that's something positive for you, at least. A banishment dies with the one who issued it, after all," he said with a neutral face.

I was taken aback by that. "I didn't like her, but I didn't want her dead."

For a moment I saw something flash in his eyes. Had that been a test? Had I passed? I didn't know, but I was alive, so I couldn't have failed too badly.

CHAPTER 19

VISIT FROM A SOLDIER

I didn't quite know what to do, so I did what I always did and retreated into my work. I couldn't stop the enemy that Isha and Atie had described. I couldn't destroy half a village in one moment, but I could get there one day.

My current project was much the same as I'd already done—to make crystals of all the colors of the rainbow. It would serve as a good exercise at the very least, practice until I could make something more potent. One by one, I worked to make the tiny particles of magic conductive material, setting them into tiny diamonds and on my wall.

There was another use for this as well, training. Over the years I'd found that uses of magic became easier as they were practiced. Fire and force were now fairly straightforward, easier, more powerful. Even if I didn't have concrete measurements, I knew that using magic made that particular magic more potent, like exercise. This was something I was keen to exploit; I would make myself stronger through hard work.

I spent days locked in my workshop, working on making more crystals, and then locking them in prisons of diamonds. Until one day I was disturbed once more. The little bell I had installed to call for me jingled, so I made my way upstairs. I wasn't fully prepared for what I saw there.

My friend Ian hadn't been around for some time, but that wasn't unusual. He was a guard, and sometimes he needed to go on long missions, but he now sat in my kitchen, and at a glance, I could see things had not gone well. Across the front of his body was a large patch of newly grown skin, much of his gut covered in pinkish flesh. Across from him, Isha was preparing some drinks, looking worried.

"Ian, what happened?" I asked when I saw him.

"Just got back from the west; war happened. They sent me home to heal up and get more gear. That's why I'm here, my friend; your armor probably saved my life." He looked sad and worried, something new for him.

Some time ago I'd made Ian armor from shells, something that would hopefully protect him if the worst came to pass, and it seemed that it had. Even if that were so, he was still sitting here, which meant that there had been at least a partial success.

"The armor?" I inquired.

"Stopped the fire long enough for me to live. I hope you don't mind, but I left it back with the others; even damaged it might save someone else's life," he said, scratching his head in slight worry as he spoke, as if I'd care about that.

"Good, then it is fulfilling its purpose. I'll see about making you some more, but when do you need it?" I asked. "Oh, and does the armor need any modifications?"

"No rush. I may look better, but the healers tell me there's still a lot underneath that will take time to fix—weeks before I'm back to my old self. The leaders also want to go over every moment of the fighting with me. Things are strange out there, Justin, very strange."

"How so?" I inquired.

Ian spent the better part of the next hour telling me how the enemy was using all kinds of new tactics. There were too many magic users, for one—far too many—but they were being used as fodder. They were weak—nothing more valuable than another soldier—and if he was judging things right, very young. The fighting was still only in the beginning stages, skirmishes here and there, but it was unbelievably violent.

What I needed was magical armor for him, but I didn't have it, and had no way to get it. I worked over some of the ideas in my head, but there were limits to what I could do. At the very least though I could make him some new armor, something to protect him again, should he end up fighting again.

When he was finished, he left and I bid him well. Then I sat there thinking for a bit, but my thoughts were disturbed. A small hand touched my arm, and suddenly I realized that Isha had come to sit with me, snuggling closely. She did this sometimes when I wasn't in my lab—during meals or breaks, though I took few of either.

"How bad is it?" she asked.

"I don't know," I answered honestly. "But I suspect it is pretty bad."

My house was now a constant place of work. Ida worked on cloth and the many arts surrounding it, struggling to make better and better pieces, to perfect the techniques so they could be taught. Chien constantly worked on ideas for tools and things that could be implemented instantly. The ideas needed to spread, and he was becoming an expert at that. Atie, for her part, had happily fallen right back into pottery, spending her days working clay into shape.

Then there was Isha. Over the last week that she'd been living with me, she'd taken on a sort of a caretaking role. Her magic was specialized toward food and small household things, and so she began to see to all of that. She went to the market to get the needed materials and foods, made sure there was always a meal if someone needed it, cleaned, and generally kept everything running smoothly. It might not have been the most glamorous of jobs, but even I could tell that it was making everyone's lives easier.

More importantly than that though was what she did at night. She'd lie down beside me, finding a crook against my chest, and fall asleep there, something which brought me unbelievable peace. It stilled my thoughts to have her with me, calmed my mind so it couldn't race, and let me rest better than I had in a long time. Nothing sexual had happened between us, but it didn't need to; being able to sleep was more than enough for me.

"Elia . . . Justin," she said as she leaned against me, still having problems with my new name.

"Yes?" I asked.

"Do you remember what you told me before you left the village?"

"I remember all of our conversations," I answered.

She was speaking now of a promise I'd made to her. I'd told her that if she joined me when my mother and father broke away that I would tell her my secrets. It had been said at the spur of the moment, but I'd meant it then, and if she asked, I'd have to decide if I was a liar or not.

"You don't need to tell me everything, but I'm worried. You spend all day locked in that room of yours, the one you won't let anyone else in, and you barely ever come out. Can you at least tell me what you're doing that's so important?"

"That isn't a secret, or at least not a big one. I'm trying to make tools that use magic," I told her. "That or better materials, but it is slow going."

"How can a tool use magic though?" she asked.

"Would you like to see?" I offered. I'd told her that I would share everything with her, and in that moment, showing her my lab seemed like such an unimportant thing.

CHAPTER 20

SHARING SECRETS

Of course Isha wanted to see my workroom. I secretly suspected that a lot of people wanted into that particular room but were too polite to ask. Nobody other than me went down there. Not Chien, not Ida, no one. But I was going to let Isha in, at least this once.

She looked on in wonder as I opened the door—a large stone construction. I'd had to replace this door multiple times already, and though it was decidedly a door, if you didn't know where it was, it would just look like a wall, another safety measure.

"You know there are lots of people who can lift that, right?" she asked as I moved the makeshift door out of the way.

"It's locked in place," I said. "If you don't push with magic on the inside in just the right places, it won't open."

"Then break it down?"

"Atal could, I'm sure, or someone else very strong, but even Larus would've had a hard time breaking down this door." It might look like stone, but the inside was far more complicated, and I had a ready source of steel nearby.

Isha let out a small chuckle as she followed me down the stairs. Oddly, stairs were fairly common in this world, though the majority were a little more oddly shaped than mine. It wasn't hard to cut things like footholds into stone with a bit of magic, so people had, and I'd done much the same with my own.

With a wave, I lit the lamps that kept this place illuminated, the small oil-soaked wicks springing to life at my call. They shone their light upon wonders that countless people in Atal have only dreamed of seeing in person—large amounts of sparkling metal, carved wood, and even my proto-computer, the copper wires now dormant as it was laid off to the side.

Generally, I expected Isha to *ooh* and *aah* over the many things I'd built and mounted on the walls all around, but she never failed to surprise me. Instead, she walked over to one of my tables and looked at it with disdain.

"What is this?" she asked, pointing to the wooden tabletop.

"A table?" The elves of this world had tables, often stone or wood blocks that had been propped up on stands; I even had a couple. Taller surfaces were often parts of whatever they were built into, like the tops of stoves or the edges of my forge. A simple wooden table wasn't normal.

"It's wood, and smooth, and tall," she pointed out, running her hand over the surface. "Very smooth. Why don't we have any of these upstairs?"

I had to stop and blink for a few moments. My house was decorated like most elven homes. There were a few low makeshift tables, enough for people to sit at and work or eat and keep their stuff off the ground, but not like this one.

"Is . . . is this important to you? Not all the, you know?" I motioned to the racks of tools and metal gadgets.

"Yes, yes Elian. I know you're fancy, but we could use these," she answered, crossing her arms over her chest. "Nobody would have to bend down to work, and these too."

She picked up the wooden stool beside that table and held it up. This was something that actually wasn't common. There were a few large stone chairs, like what Atal used for a throne, but wooden stools like this weren't common, as most people just sat on the ground.

"They're for sitting on, right?" Isha asked.

"Uh, yeah?" I was a bit confused by the direction this was going.

She tried it out, plopping down on the stool and placing her hands on the table, looking quite satisfied with the result.

"Do you have any more things like this? Wait, where do you sleep down here? I know you do sometimes." Her thoughts were not at all what I'd expected, so I just pointed her to the bed I had. It was a rope bed, piled up with some leather cushions filled with soft plant matter. She promptly laid down there too, ignoring the fact that I was getting more and more flustered by the moment.

"Isha?" I said tiredly.

"One of these, too, I want one of these. Why would you not build one of these upstairs? It's so soft! That doesn't make any sense, Elian!" We still slept piled up in a shaped section of limbs and boughs, which had its own charm, in my opinion. Apparently, my opinion was wrong.

"Isha, I didn't bring you down here to show you furniture. I brought you to show you my work."

"You have no idea," she answered, marching up to me and poking me in the chest with her tiny pointer finger. "You don't know what things you make are impressive because you're always off in your own head. Sure, you can make lots and lots of pretty things that do work, but we can use *these*, right now," she said, motioning to the table, stools, and the bed. "Nobody would even want to steal them, and we wouldn't need to hide them or anything, like you do. Did that even occur to you?"

"I . . . perhaps I should think more about what I share, but these aren't important to me, so I never did," I answered after a few moments. "They seem normal, so I ignored them."

"Now that you're thinking, share the normal things you think of more often. What was it you thought I would *want* to see?" she asked.

Slightly relieved, I showed her a few of my tools. Those were not all that interesting to her, but she did look harder at the various samples of materials beside them. There was really nothing like sulfur or aluminum, the latter of which got a lot of attention, because it was shiny.

Though the most attention was given to the diamonds I had sitting there, with Isha picking one up and spinning it in the light.

"I thought you might like those," I chuckled.

"You could buy anything you want with these," she answered, shaking her head. "But you don't care, do you?"

"Not really."

Isha totally ignored the computer, more interested in the copper wire than in what it was doing when I showed her.

"So what, it can count? Does it do anything else?"

"Not currently, but it could. In time I could make it do all kinds of interesting things—make math easy, answer complex questions, work through massive amounts of information in seconds." She just gave me a blank look.

"But it just counts? I like the copper string though. Can I have some?" Her words wounded me deeply. Perhaps in time she'd come to see how cool computers were, but not today, it seemed.

"Wire, and yes, I'll give you some." That would be easy enough to explain, and there were a few fun things she could probably do with it.

"Thank you. Does it really need a different word though?"

"Yes, yes it does, and it is called wire." My unhappy response got her to put her hands up placatingly.

Finally, I took her to my latest project, something that, even if she didn't understand, I hoped she would like. I'd put a lot of work into these, a massive quantity of magic for each one. The little rack that held the grain-sized mana crystals suspended in diamonds shone when I pushed a bit of my magic into it.

"Pretty, I like these better than most lights." After checking with me first, she picked one up, and I could see her push some magic into the small crystal, the center of it beginning to shine with a soft yellow light.

"Glad I finally made something that impresses you," I joked.

Isha put down the little rock and wrapped her arms around my neck, pulling me closer until our lips met.

"You impress me all the time, just not always in the ways you think," she said softly.

"I'm glad to hear that," I smirked, kissing her again.

"You know, since you're sharing things with me, there's something I'd like to show you too." With a quick series of pulls, the ties holding her dress fell away, the garment fluttering to the floor. "We just needed somewhere private."

With a little tug, she led me to the small bed, her eyes smiling as she pulled me down with her.

CHAPTER 21

WRITING

Things changed slowly around my home. I brought in more things that were normal to me, but still odd to others. These were often things that I didn't really think about, things that I'd never considered as important to the world. Decorations, cabinets, holders for various things here and there. None of them were large, but all of them were something, and they all mattered in their own small way.

Then I invented something that I had put off for a long time, one that I was deeply afraid others wouldn't see the need for, but which I was sure would play an important role in this world. Stripped bark from a specific type of tree lay before me in small sheets, and a small stick of charcoal. It was time to work on proper writing.

There were a few written systems for record keeping and the like, but they were painfully basic. They tended to be very limited in scope. You couldn't, for instance, write a novel, or even an instruction book, because the language mechanics just couldn't handle that. They were even limited on the math they performed, not that many people did math beyond multiplication and division anyway.

Armed with my newfound materials, I sat down and began my first draft. I was by no means a linguist, but there were things I could do. For instance, I could translate the Atali dialect of our tongue into a phonetic alphabet, with punctuation for basic grammar and speech conventions. I could've used the basic English alphabet, but that seemed dangerous. There was no evidence that I was the only, or would be, the only transmigrator, so keeping English in my back pocket for someone who might come along could one day be useful. So, I made a few simple symbols and assigned them sounds, building from there.

It had been a few weeks since Isha and Atie had joined me, a few long weeks. There were whispers and rumors of war and large orders for me to process and send out, but since my interaction with Isha down in my lab and the subsequent change in our relationship, I'd taken up a new hobby. Every day I needed to try and implement something from my old world that I found convenient. It didn't need to be big, and shouldn't be too complex, just something small to improve our lives. Writing was today's project.

Creating a written language might seem like a massive undertaking, but the language itself already existed; I was just making a complementary alphabet. Using what I knew about Korean and the Japanese kana, mixed with a bit of my own native tongue for structure, I came up with something that was quick and easy to learn. I even included a symbol for sarcasm. Though, as I thought about it, quick and easy was perhaps not needed, with our memories being what they were. I could still recite all the things Atal's granddaughter had told me weeks ago verbatim, and everything I'd learned from fourth grade in my previous life. It was very odd.

As the sun began to set, I called in my house companions to get their opinions. I ran through the alphabet quickly, showing them how each letter represented a sound and explained the basic grammar structure.

"How do you know if the person you're talking to is to be respected or not? You didn't include any markings for the tone there," Chien said first.

In our current tongue, there were tones that one might use to indicate respect, like that of elders, along with word choice. They weren't always different words per se, but more of how things were said, like putting emphasis on a given word.

"It shouldn't need that," I said.

"No, it absolutely does. If you did this and wrote a letter to an elder without showing respect, they'd be livid, especially if it looked the same for a slave," Atie added. Ida nodded in agreement, and given her perspective, her opinion carried weight.

"Is it one of those symbols?" Isha asked, pointing to the page that had the math written on it.

"Um, no, those are for math."

"Seriously? How much math do we really need? You only need to count and stuff, right?" Chien said with a shake of his head.

"You need a lot."

"Like what?" he continued.

"Like being able to add, subtract, divide something into multiple parts, repeat something multiple times, and a whole host of other things." I really didn't want to go deep into math right now.

"There are too many symbols for that," Chien griped, not letting it drop. "What are the rest for?"

"All right, pretend there's a perfect circle . . ." We spent the next five minutes finding the area under a curve in part of that circle, at which point they all looked at me like I was mad.

"So . . . it just keeps going infinitely, and you can do that?" Chien now looked deeply confused, which made sense, because he'd missed a lot of math before calculus.

"I mean, the world doesn't work like that perfectly. There are smallest units, probably, but it works for a lot of stuff." If they tried to get me going on physics, I would ardently refuse, but it seemed, at least, that Chien was now willing to drop it.

"Is . . . is this how you see the world?" Isha asked.

"Sort of? I mean, I don't go around measuring everything all the time or doing the equations, but I know they're there. Like I said, the math doesn't work perfectly for the world, probably." I knew a lot, but I also knew I didn't know everything, and it was good to acknowledge that.

"No wonder he seems insane half the time," Atie said with a shake of her head.

"You know, we should begin teaching you some of this, Chien."

"Pass," the young man said.

"Seriously?"

"Hard pass. I don't see the point in any of it." His statement echoed those of kids all throughout my previous life, even me. I knew that one day he would understand at least the point of some of the knowledge I could impart, and with magic like mine, he could probably use it, but until he saw it, I wouldn't insist.

"Well, I'd like to learn, and when your friend Ian returns again, perhaps he will too," Atie said with a smirk. They'd only met once or twice, but I got the feeling she might like him.

I worried about Ian, but I'd done all I could for him. He'd come to me for new armor, and I had delivered. Rather than using shells for it this time, I went a different direction. Ida's work on fabric had been rough but perfect for what I had in mind. Instead of carving the shells that could turn brittle or break easily, I'd taken a lot of her failed pieces and layered them, a simple glue forming them into hardened sheets. I'd even hidden small steel wires in some of them to protect the vital areas of the torso and for added strength. The new armor was just as light and much stronger than its predecessor.

"All right, Auntie. I'll be more than happy to teach you, whenever I find free time."

"Good luck on that one," Chien laughed.

CHAPTER 22

CALL TO ARMS

I'd just started running my aunt through the basics of algebra when a visitor arrived at my door. Those were getting more and more common these days—either orders from the local government for weapons or more craftsmen who needed to be taught things. It seemed I didn't have, and wouldn't have, any free time in the near future.

"What today?" I asked the young man at my door. I recognized him as one of the runners for the local powers that be.

"Atal wishes to see you," he said simply, and that was it.

Who knew what he wanted. Did he desire more weapons? Then he would have them. More spears for his men? I'd do what I could. While iron was fairly common and I'd had quite a lot, there was a limit to my current availability. But if Atal wanted it, I'd gladly hand it over to see the people who destroyed my home gone. Perhaps that was foolish, since I knew he was at best dangerous and at worst an uncaring madman, but I had to work with what I had.

Knowing that my 'boss' wasn't one to be kept waiting, I left as quickly as I could. There were improvements everywhere at the palace. Arches were springing up in various place, as were the beginnings of cement use and a few tools that I'd designed. It was gratifying to see my work here, even if the progress was still ongoing.

I was pleased that my guide didn't take me to the throne room or any of the formal areas. Instead, he brought me to a field, where a number of soldiers were practicing. Elders moved among the men, correcting postures and giving instruction where needed. I could also see a number of magic users working on their arts as well. Above it all was Atal, who was looking out at them intently.

"Greetings, Ancient," I said as I approached, bowing slightly.

"Justin, I'm glad you're here. As you can see, some of your newer weapons have been distributed, as well as the armor," he said as he gestured at a couple of elves who I could barely follow. As they were striking at each other and their weapons met, ringing sounds made their way up to where I was standing with Atal. I could tell as they slowed down that at least they were using practice weapons and not the much nicer ones.

"I am glad to see it," I said. "Do you think they will be enough for what you have planned?" It was clear he was up to something.

"Perhaps, perhaps not. The reports I've received over the last few days tell me of an enemy who is sweeping quickly through small villages, leaving little in their wake. That is why I am going with these soldiers." Few times had I seen him look like he actually cared, or display much concern at all really, but he did now.

"I've given you what I could manage, Ancient, but if you think there's something more I can do, please tell me."

That wasn't a lie either. The weapons I could reliably reproduce had been brought to him. One day I could manage cannons or something, but the testing involved would be extensive, and I really didn't trust anyone else with explosives at this time. They had the best I could make in the time I'd been provided. Even something like a ballista or trebuchet would take knowledge and buildup that I just didn't have yet.

"There is something, but not an item. I wish you to join us, to see what is happening and to think on your feet while you're out there with us. You've proven yourself able to come up with solutions before, and I would see to it that you have everything you need." His tone implied that this was less a request and more of a demand.

"Me?"

"Yes."

"I've never been on a battlefield," I said, unsure of what I would be doing.

"Yet you've seen the monsters before, the ones I suspect our enemies are creating, and you fought one, and won. Few of my soldiers have managed that. We fight each other so little that real experience of that kind isn't to be underestimated. A monster? Certainly! I have dozens I could send without issue, but another group of elves? Other than myself and a few of the older ones, none have fought like this." That made sense. While there were conflicts, war wasn't common.

"I understand," I said, knowing that arguing further wouldn't help. "Is there anything you wish me to bring?"

"Whatever you think you'll need. We leave at sundown," he said.

Once I was dismissed I rushed home. I had only a few hours to prepare and no idea exactly what to bring. While I'd made plenty of weapons, and some would be coming with me, I wasn't a soldier. On my way back home, I considered throwing some armor together but quickly dismissed it. The extra weight would slow me down, and if I ended up on the front line, something would be going wrong anyway.

When I got to my door, I also considered the worst possibility—that this could be an attempt by Atal to either test or discard me. He could, with ease, put me in a situation where I would die and he would look blameless, but would he? From what I'd seen, Atal could also just kill me outright and there'd be little anyone could do about it, but it might dissuade Chien from helping him, and perhaps . . . No, if I thought like that too much, I might end up making things worse, and it wouldn't help anyway. I just needed to be prepared for everything; then it would be fine.

Isha saw me come in the door and immediately understood that something was going on.

"Elian, what's wrong?" she asked, instantly on edge.

"I need to pack. Atal has called me to join him on a mission," I explained in as few words as possible.

"Where?" she said as she followed me.

"The invaders who destroyed our home are still around. I think he plans to resolve the issue, and he wants me to join him." I was throwing some food and water-skins into a small leather satchel as I spoke, barely looking up.

"Don't go," Isha said, pain leaking into her voice.

"I don't have much of a choice."

"There is always a choice; don't go," she repeated. "What if something happens to you?"

"It could," I answered truthfully, turning to look at her. She'd taken up a position in the door, as if to block me from leaving. "Something could happen anywhere, but if I don't go, I know what will happen. First, we'd have to flee the city, at least, and they'd search for me. Then, when I got somewhere else, something could happen, someone else could decide they wanted my work and then what? We're back here again."

"You're the only one who knows how to work iron," she objected.

"A good reason for Atal to keep me safe," I responded, but even as I did, I looked for the little book of tree bark I'd made and began to write. "Before I go though, I will do something about that."

I furiously scribbled instructions. Only a few people knew my writing system to any degree, and though it was still a work in progress, something like this would be good enough. Some of the grammar and tone symbology and rules hadn't been worked out yet, but directions? It would serve. When I was done, I held it out to her, but she ardently refused to accept it.

"If something happens," I said, pushing it against her crossed arms.

"Fine, but if you don't come back, I'll hunt you down," she said after a brief standoff.

"Well, that might be the best reason I've heard to return yet," I replied with a smirk, only for the book to be swung at me.

CHAPTER 23

FIRST BATTLE

The sun crept over the horizon on the third day of our trip from Atal—the city—and Atal—the man—was acting more and more anxious by the mile. It was hard to see, stoic as he tended to be, but he was always calling for scouts to check on something, always making sure our watchmen were on point. I was glad for that because it showed he knew to expect issues, but it was also tiring, even for me, and I wasn't on watch.

We were still far from the furthest edges of the territory, but we were moving fast. Normally one would expect that a group would move far slower than an individual might, but in this case it wasn't so. There was little in the way of luggage, and the fact that we had people with us who knew the land like the backs of their hands meant that we never got lost and took the best trails.

Twice on this trip we'd stopped in villages on the way, but there was nothing of note except the way they dealt with us. Normally it was the village's elder who was the most respected, who demanded what they wanted, but Atal was with us, as were some of his subordinates, and this changed the equation. Both elders in the villages had come out to greet us, speaking humbly and offering anything we might need or want. Our leader, though, had waved them off, happy to get the information he wanted and keep going.

The information was . . . not good. While nobody had spotted enemies in this area yet, there were a few—and only a few—refugees coming from further west. It appeared that they weren't killing everyone in the villages when they attacked—just the older and stronger people, the ones who posed a threat.

Around noon we crested a small rise and looked down on a new village. In an instant I could tell something was wrong, but I couldn't put my finger on it. Fortunately others were with me, and they too sensed the wrongness; within seconds word had been spread all through our war party. We had over a hundred elves ready to fight in an instant, all turning their eyes toward the settlement.

Like a bolt of lightning, it hit me. There was no movement, none at all. Even as I looked at the houses, I saw more and more that was wrong. There was no smoke, no cooking fires, no gathering parties out and about. In a few places, even the leaves looked like they had just grown in. Everything seemed . . . repaired.

It was when these flaws registered in my mind that the first attack began. A dozen or more spears arced toward the center of our line, the image of them coming at us barely a blur as they screamed out from the forest. I would like to say that I was ready, throwing up shields and stopping the attack, but I wasn't. I wasn't a soldier; I wasn't trained or prepared for that first attack, and it might have killed me.

Those around me were though. Without delay, spells sprang into place, and projectiles were knocked from the air. Atal, who'd been the primary target, was a blur himself as he struck out, ripping the teeth from the assault. Our enemy might have come to fight, but so had we.

"Fire!" a nearby man screamed, pointing, and this time I was ready.

I snapped a barrier up, upon which splashed a wave of burning heat, exploding well before it got to our lines. Fire was one of my go-to spells, and dealing with it was as easy as pie. I even had time to issue a response in the form of a blade of force, shooting forward in a killing line.

The assault came hard and fast, the enemy's back line hurling spears and large spells while their front line also charged. There were so many casters, and as I looked out before me, I realized why. Each of the front liners moving in our direction had the same kind of aura, and one ran through with burning veins; they were expending their energy and their lives to kill us.

A skilled military historian from Earth might have been able to follow what was happening, but I doubted anything in my previous world's history matched up to what we were seeing here. It was a chaos of magic and spears, steeped with ancient weapons and tactics. Many of the fighters squared off in small groups, keeping no cohesive formation while others just rained down chaos on both sides.

I and most of the soldiers were floundering, unable to process the differences between the fighting of men and monsters the center held. Enough of the older elves around our leader had seen combat like this, and I had no doubt that the oldest was well versed himself. Enemies broke on them like water on the shore, throwing them back with force.

There was no time to watch, though, as I had to duck under a spear of energy thrown in my direction. Even as I dodged it, the man behind me didn't, and I heard his scream of pain as it ripped a sizzling hole in him. There were no words, no speaking beyond screams of anger and pain.

One of their scouts crested our hill and began to fly upward, hands covered in deadly looking power. With a flick, I sent forth another blade, slicing his appendages from him before he fell, not ten feet in front of us screaming. The scream was so . . . high pitched, that I couldn't resist looking.

At that moment, I realized with horror that these weren't men we were fighting; they were boys. The one I'd just cut down couldn't be more than fifteen. It sent a chill down my spine as the blood flowed from his stumps and onto the ground, his life force draining before me. There was no sense in it, to sacrifice the young like this. It was appalling, particularly toward a people who often viewed their children as protectively as we did.

While I'd killed one, Atal was killing in droves. The spears I'd given him each turned into a line of death through the enemy formation, ripping and tearing and leaving little more than gore in their wake. Each stone from the ball thrower was like a cannon shot, leaving a crater and sending those around it to the ground as shrapnel ripped into them. The enemy force was smaller than ours, and they'd greatly underestimated us.

In less than a minute we'd advanced, pushing their line back as the child soldiers fell in droves and their back line cracked under the weight of the older elves' assault. I made it to the boy I'd cut down, where he lay crying on the ground. He'd managed to cauterize the stumps, but he was still fading fast.

"Why?" I asked him, not bothering to keep the pain from my voice.

"They have my mom, my sisters," he wept. "Said if I didn't, they'd . . ." The last was drowned out by a groan of pain, but I could well guess what he was going to say next.

All around me, more of the surviving children began to immolate, exploding outward like bombs.

"I'm sorry," the boy said, and I felt magic grip my body so I couldn't flee. "I have to." I could feel the heat building, growing into a small bomb.

"Me too," I replied, before sending an arrow of force into his skull, killing him instantly. "Sleep, child. I hope you find peace."

As I looked up, I saw the back line of the enemy force coalesce around a single point and begin pushing forward. It seemed the monsters we were after had finally decided to meet us head on. Spells were exchanged, but soon they drew close enough that I could see their leader, and I was flabbergasted.

The girl they were all moving around had ice-cold eyes and a sneer of anger as she advanced, lips and body moving in some sort of song and dance that sent waves of power outward. A few of the men were singing too, though there was enough difference in dialect that it was hard to understand their words. The intent though was clear; this was a song of war.

Before long, their dancing general had made her way to the front of the line. Her dress was short, far shorter than what most of our people wore, and her hair was white, all except for a single streak of red that hung down by her face. It was odd, seeing such a beauty exuding so much hate, but she did, and she was coming.

CHAPTER 24

DEATHS

All around me the battle raged. There were the screams of elves dying and suffering as they were burned. I was unprepared for this. How could I have ever been? How could I have thought that this would be all right? Clearly it wasn't. We'd been ambushed, brought into a fight that we should have expected.

While I was trying to shield myself and return fire with some of the child soldiers, Atal and the woman who was leading the enemy began their battle. I wanted to look, to see what they were doing, but there was no time.

Two more of the child soldiers screamed, charging at my unit, hands ablaze with magical energy. Perhaps they had power, lots of it, but they had no idea how to use it. I tried not to weep as I tossed out bolts of force, caving in the chests of innocent victims. For I had to remember that that was who we were fighting, children who'd been forced to fight.

Another appeared, but this time an adult—one of the handlers, I supposed. He also lacked the burning aura, though still had some magic, as the spear he threw at me flew at superhuman speed. Unfortunately for him, I was already in the process of fighting, and walls of force were a specialty of mine. The projectile shattered like glass against such a barrier.

This enemy saw that I was no pushover and tried to retreat, jumping backward. It was a foolish move. I managed to catch him in midair. Weeks back, something had occurred to me while I was thinking about how to fight Atal. Those with physical magics needed something to apply force against. At the time, I'd considered the possibility of just throwing Atal into space, though who knew if that would work.

Such methods weren't needed for this lesser specimen though. Once he was off the ground and unable to do anything about it, I simply wrapped a cord of energy around his neck and pulled hard, popping his head off like a wine cork. It was horrible to watch, but this act caused the enemies in view to pause for a moment and reorient themselves. Some clearly wanted to flee my presence; others turned toward me and charged.

Among those who wished to fight me was an elf with a small amount of white in his hair. That wasn't good. In a fight against an elder, I was sure to lose. He began to gather a truly massive amount of fire, while a couple of others covered him, the orb growing by the second. Perhaps it was time to pull more tricks out?

Other than fire and force, I'd also been working on light. I knew of at least a few ways to weaponize it. I cupped my hands, and an instant flash blazed within them, like I'd used against those thieves what seemed like years ago. I followed up with more of the same, because if I could make light bright enough to make steel glow, I could make light bright enough to cook flesh.

Assuming my enemy wasn't a complete fool and had some form of shield like my own, I sent a laser right at him—a potent beam that struck the middle of his chest and ripped it open. This kind of thing wouldn't be useful long range, but for close combat, it certainly was. It was horrid to watch the other elf burn, but I had no choice if I wanted to return to Isha.

My target's magic didn't go away though. It seemed that dropping him in the middle of his spell caused the thing to go critical and explode, sending fire across their lines and a blast wave that tossed many of the disoriented elves like rag dolls.

An instant later I felt stone hands grip me, and my world briefly turned to a blur before I blacked out.

There was no time to respond, no chance to move, just a blur and nothing. I didn't know how long had passed when I came to, but I saw one of our healers standing over me, hands outstretched. I looked to be behind some rock. Though based on the sounds, the battle was still raging.

"What . . ." I said as I tried to rise.

"You managed to get the enemy leader to look at you. Atal wasn't able to be gentle when he pulled you out. Most people aren't meant to move that fast, Justin, so stay down a second while I make sure you're okay."

"How are things?" I asked, since I could still hear what was going on around us.

"The old ones are still fighting it out. Not going well," he said. "The enemy sent someone strong."

Before he could say much more, our general showed up. Atal landed near us, and the area around him was hammered by something I couldn't see. Along with this came a loud noise, like a sharp scream.

"What is it?" I yelled as the attack began to fade.

"She uses her voice," Atal responded. "Need to take out her aides, but can't get to them. Any ideas?" For the first time ever, the ancient seemed genuinely worried. Normally Atal was unflappable, but now there was sweat on his brow and a few cuts that looked like actual injuries.

I was somewhat charmed that he'd ask me such a thing, and yes, I did have ideas. I'd not really considered fighting Isha in the past, but I had thought about what she'd told me of the man who destroyed our village, and it seemed that this woman used a similar technique—a very loud sound. A very loud sound could destroy.

"I'll need a moment to set up, approach from behind," I said before Atal disappeared again.

Bringing my hands up, I began to write a new spell into the world. It was based largely on what I'd already done, just an expansion. This was easier than creating a completely new spell, which I'd struggle to put together properly.

Walls of force snapped into place, layered one over another, and then I began to empty the space between. A vacuum of sorts, an area devoid of air. It would be a risk. I didn't know if this magic worked just as I thought it did, but the idea was to block sound. I didn't even believe it would last for too long, but it didn't need to—just long enough.

Once my sound shield was formed, I popped out from behind the rock to get a look at what was going on. Within a moment, it was clear where the problems lay. Across from us the female elf was still dancing, still moving, all around her a net-like shield spread, covering her and the chorus of men, joining in her song of death. My goal here would be to isolate her, surprise her, get them all off balance just long enough for Atal to strike.

This was aided by the fact that as soon as she saw me, a wicked gleam shone in her eyes and she sent a scream in my direction, scouring the land like a fierce wind. Well, it battered everything until it hit my shield. The first wall broke quickly, but that mattered little. The tiny voids I'd created with my spell could not transmit sound; there was nothing to carry it forward. Sure, the outer layers of my barrier spell broke, but I could just make more and more voids.

The elven woman's eyes grew big as she saw me standing there unharmed, and she screamed harder. I couldn't hear it, isolated as I was from the outside world, but I could see her strain. As soon as she stopped, I smiled. I began the same process again, but this time I built it around her. As fast as I could, I repeated the spell, building layers of insulation around her, isolating her from her cronies.

It didn't take long for panic to spread among her people. Several of the soldiers stopped when they could no longer hear their leader's voice, and they turned toward her. Spells faltered as the magic keeping them going was interrupted. In time, they could have responded properly— reformed, remade their defenses—but they didn't have time.

That moment of weakness was enough for Atal to make his way through their forces. I couldn't follow him, couldn't see him, but I could see the effects of his movement. Where once stood men were now clouds of blood and gore, bodies exploding as the angry ancient ripped people apart. When it was over, he stood still, alone, directly in front of the siren.

"Will that barrier harm me?" he shouted back at me, not even looking.

"Shouldn't," I replied.

A moment later it shattered like spun glass, and Atal appeared beside the female leader, his hand around her throat. As he lifted her into the air, it dawned on her that she'd lost, but the ancient didn't rip or tear, didn't rend her like he had so many already; instead, he seemed to merely squeeze.

It took only a second for our enemy to discern his intent, and then she began struggling like a fish on a hook. Without breath she couldn't sing, couldn't scream, couldn't respond as he lifted her higher into the air and watched her struggle. The battle, which moments ago had been a riot of sound and movement, was now frozen, her gagging and struggles as the furious ancient slowly strangled her the only noise, as her hands and feet lashed out against him uselessly.

The process wasn't fast, and after a few moments she stopped. Instead of trying to claw or strike at Atal, her eyes watered as she put her hands up in a pleading gesture. It was impressive how quickly she realized her situation, and how she tried to change it in the only way she knew. Atal was unmoved at her open hands, her desperate tapping of his arm, even as she failingly reached for him, unable to reach since his arms were long.

There was more struggling when it became apparent that Atal had no intention of giving her mercy, but it didn't last. Powerless as the singer now was, she slowly weakened, body shaking and then going limp. For a few moments more, I watched as Atal held her there, before his hand moved, sending a cracking sound across the battlefield—the breaking of her neck—and he threw the broken body to the side.

I approached, unable to take my eyes off the results. Blood was everywhere, mixed with broken bodies and singed ground. In the center of it all stood Atal, over the body of his defeated counterpart. The woman's eyes, tinged with red, stared up at me, empty. It was odd, so odd to see someone so beautiful so broken, but I quickly reminded myself of the children she'd led into battle and what had been done to them. That quelled any stirrings of pity. She'd been pretty, and people liked pretty things, but she'd been party to so much evil.

"Good work," Atal said, finally turning to me. "We should go over what happened here before we return. I have a feeling we'll need more soldiers."

CHAPTER 25

FIRST FORT

A tal waited until we'd returned to the last village we'd visited to speak with me, for which I was grateful, as it gave me time to organize my thoughts. He was as distant as always, but a few times I caught him looking at me, watching me. Surely something was on his mind.

The two of us found a hut, and others were banished from it. He wouldn't even allow anyone near it. Atal clearly wanted privacy.

"That shield, what was it?" he asked, eyes reflecting the small fire between us.

"Layers, with nothing in between, or as near to nothing as I could manage," I answered truthfully.

"Nothing? Just layers? Justin, this makes no sense. That woman was far more powerful than you. She should have easily destroyed any defense you created. I should have been the only one to leave that battlefield when it was over." He didn't say this as if he'd wanted it, or desired it. Just matter of fact; that was how things were.

After some consideration, I came to the conclusion that he was probably right too. That woman wasn't as strong as he was, and in time he might have won, but the rest of us? No, we'd probably be dead, at least more of us than there already were. Perhaps even all of us by the time it was done.

"Think . . . like the ocean—that is what sound is like," I explained. "There is stuff in the air, stuff that carries it. By removing that stuff, there was nothing for her sound to move, so it stopped. Eventually more stuff reached it, but until then the barrier held."

As I explained, I made a small illusion—just lines and dots. It was primitive, but perhaps something he could follow without more explanation.

"Stuff in the air? Nonsense, there is nothing there," the ancient objected.

"Then what is wind?" I asked.

That set him to thinking for a long time.

"The air is like water?" he asked.

"Sort of," I said. "Much thinner of course, but much like water. You could say that birds are swimming in it like fish do in the ocean. It is much the same."

Now he fixed me with an appraising look. "How do you know this? My father told me when I was young that birds flew because it was their nature, like we build and speak. Who told you different? Not your village, for I knew Elaya, and she held no such beliefs. I knew her long before you were born."

Crap. Part of the problem with elves that lived for literal centuries was that if they lived even remotely near one another, there was a good chance they knew each other. Perhaps he hadn't spoken with Elaya in fifty years, but with our memories, it wouldn't matter. Did I lie and perhaps gain his ire? Perhaps a partial truth then.

"There are some secrets I wish to keep, but once, a long time ago I ate a piece of fruit, one I'd never seen before or since. It was foolish, but I had my reasons, and it changed things. It made me change, and because of it, I see things differently."

I waited as he watched me, trying not to sweat under the gaze of an ancient monster who could rip me apart. Eventually all things came together, though, and he sighed.

"Boy, you are a thousand years too young to lie to me, but you're lucky I like you. Well, 'like' is perhaps strong, but you are useful. The how and why of your abilities are secondary to me right now. I need the what, as in, what do you know that can help push back this invasion?" It wasn't lost on me that he had said 'right now,' but that was something.

"There are things we could do to protect the villages, but I think that's not our first concern. They're using children, which means they don't have enough soldiers. From what one of them said, they're holding the soldiers' families captive. If we free them, we've turned half of their people or more." That was the first thought I had, though there were others.

"Agreed. They are desperate; the woman they sent was the clearest indication of that." For a moment I looked at him and he explained. "I am here because these are my lands, but her? She should be at home. Children born to strong parents tend to be stronger—not by much, but by enough—and it is always females who limit growth, not those like you and me. Sending her here meant they couldn't field another potent commander for this area, not that they didn't want to."

"You think they'd do that?"

"I once tried to have as many children as I could in a year. Do you know how many I managed?" he asked. That was surprising, but not alarming. After all, many men throughout my own earthly history with power like his were womanizers, and I knew he could have about as many as he wanted. "Eight. Impressive, I know, and it took me all year doing almost nothing else. It was only because I had many women that I managed such an insane number. Though admittedly afterward, I lost most of my taste for them."

"Eight." That seemed really low, even with our low birth rates.

"That reaction there, you're not surprised at all. One day I'll have to find out why," he said with half a smile.

I needed to change the subject, and now. "As for things we can do for the villages," I said as I began to draw some designs in the dirt. "We can make quick and easy walls like this, just logs with dirt piled behind them. It won't stop the enemy for long, but even a few moments. We can also build higher places to watch from, where fires can be lit if something happens. That will at least let us know that something is wrong. How close they got to here without anyone knowing was not good." He knew of walls, of course, but the design was different from what was used in the city, though as far as I knew, nobody used towers for communication or watching. Trees perhaps, or high places, but not structures.

"Good, what about something to fight with?" he asked.

"Those slings I made are easy and quick. They're not as good as powerful people, but a rock to the head kills almost anyone who isn't prepared for it, or who isn't like you," I reasoned.

"See, this is why I brought you along, Justin. Now, let's rest. Tomorrow you're going to teach the people here how to do those things."

The next day was a rush, a mad one. I needed to get people working early and fast, not something that meshed well with the very laid-back lifestyle that most lived. Magic helped, a lot, and with the number of powerful magic users we had on hand, much of the work could be brute-forced quickly.

Slings were the easiest part—just a straight stick with notches and some twine, and you could make one in under an hour. I showed them, pointing out the issues they might come upon. It would take them a long time to get good, but a stone baseball was still a stone baseball, and it could kill one of the child soldiers we'd fought yesterday.

Then came the walls, and here magic was key. It was just a berm, as simple as I could make it, and wouldn't stand up to much, but mere seconds might save lives. It would at least give people something to hide behind that might be able to stop spells. Most of our enemy's magic users weren't all that experienced, so it should work.

Finally we worked on the tower, and I was reminded once more of my many lacking skills. I wasn't an architect, and this thing needed to be built high enough to see over the trees. Unsure, I just put in as many supports as seemed reasonable and hoped for the best, because that was all I had. It stood in the village's clearing, with a fire on top to light in emergencies. Heck, not knowing what it was for, our enemy might burn it down, which would work just as well. Smoke would be visible a long way off during the day, and a high flaming light at night would serve the same purpose. If every village had one, perhaps one of their neighbors could see it, if it was high enough.

The whole time I was watched by one of the many other fighters Atal had brought with us, and I was watched by Atal himself. They were examining me, grading me, seeing what I could do. I didn't know if I passed their test or not in the end, but I was satisfied by the end of the day that I'd done what I could.

CHAPTER 26

ON WAR

There was no sense of satisfaction when I left the little village behind, no sense that everything would be okay, but I'd done all I could. We had other villages to check, other places to make sure were well before we returned to the city. And with enemies moving as fast as they were, we had little time to do it. As we moved, my mind raced through everything I knew about military tactics and methods, which wasn't much.

Sure, I'd read *The Art of War* once or twice, and there were a few things in it that might be applicable to the current conflict, but the book didn't have clear instructions for what I needed. I hadn't been much of a history buff or into medievalism, or anything like that, so I lacked a lot of knowledge on how to make tools and weapons for war in this world. For example, making a bow was beyond me, though when I got home, bows, arrows, and siege engines were decidedly on the list of items to make.

"You're thinking again," Atal said as he slid up beside me.

"That easy to tell?" I asked. "Yes, about war."

"What does a child such as you know of war?" he didn't laugh.

"To be truthful, not much. But we're in a war now, so I need to think on it. We know what they've taken, and that they're desperate, but little else."

"True, there wasn't even an attempt at speaking to us, which is odd." He didn't elaborate, and being that I didn't know our enemy as well as he probably did, I supposed he might anticipate my wanting him to.

"Would he normally? What is he like? What are his goals, if not just the pool? How many does he have? Where are they getting in at? I think if we want to win, we need to know these things." I clicked my tongue. "More importantly, why is he so desperate?"

"Good questions, and I will send people to see what we can learn— those skilled in sneaking and watching. That isn't why I brought you here though. I brought you to see what tools we might use to win, not for a strategy."

I wanted to argue, but there was an undeniable fact—Atal knew more about conducting a war in this world than I did, perhaps more than I ever would. He was old, and while I didn't know how old, I knew he was ancient; hence the way I addressed him sometimes. In that time he must have seen many wars, and many types of war.

"True, but without knowing what we're doing, at least generally, I won't know what to build." That statement got a decent silence.

"There are," Atal began after a time, "generally three ways to conduct a war. The most common is to challenge the ruler directly. If you wish to take the lands and power of one of ours, you can go to him and issue your challenge. The loser often dies; though, in some cases, they are spared, and the winner takes the holdings. This is what you do if you want to possess what your enemy has without destroying it."

That sounded like a ceremonial fight, and was probably what would end up best for the people involved in this battle. Even in the short battles I'd seen, I could see how our strongest fighting could cause destruction, and if they died, the people would be left without defense against the monsters of this world. That would be a bad proposition.

"If there is some issue that does not require such things, a dispute over a small area of land, or some resource, then a man is sent to speak to the other ruler. In the case that some agreement can be made, it is, but if not, the rules of conflict are agreed upon. It makes no sense to destroy what you want while trying to take it, no?"

That sounded more ceremonial than what happened on Earth, but closer. Normally, countries would have some limits they agreed upon, even if they were often violated. Few were willing to risk nuclear, biological, or chemical warfare. The last of which I might even be able to manage, if I were a complete maniac. Making something very nasty to spread over the enemy forces would be all too easy, but it made me cringe.

"Finally, there is what Cino is doing here. He's planning to destroy us completely. They will spread over the land and leave little behind them." It was the first time I'd heard the name of the enemy ancient, something I filed away for later. "They will dig in over the coming rainy season and attack again once the rains stop."

The winters in this land were rare, severe, and long lasting, but the normal year had a rainy season. Perhaps that had to do with magic, or some odd weather effect. I didn't know, but it made sense that they would wait while the rains came down. Even if moving about locally wasn't too bad, the daily downpours would turn paths to mud and make getting lost easier.

"Is that what they expect us to do?" I asked.

"Yes, because we have the same issues they do." His answer was accompanied by a slightly raised eyebrow.

"Then that is what we must absolutely not do. If he wishes to destroy the land, so be it, but we beat him to it. And while he tries to dig in, we destroy his sources of food, of water, even shelter if we can. We make his army suffer. There are some things we can try, some ideas I have, but someone with power could probably destroy the vines and tubers he'll need better than I could. As for digging in, well, we'll have to get to work on that soon. I have many ideas."

Atal stopped and looked at me. "If we destroy their food, they'll go further for it, and harm others."

"Then we make sure that the others they'd go for are protected. Hunger is a weapon, as sharp as a spear," I answered.

"That amount of hunger will not kill them. They will have enough to survive it."

With powerful singers to summon food and the druid-like casters to grow more, they would surely survive. That said, they wouldn't survive well; they'd be hungry, tired, angry, and quick to make mistakes.

"True, but we don't need to kill them. We need to destroy their ability to fight and their will to do so. The best we could hope for would be sending them back without ever raising a spear, but I fear that won't be possible." The more I thought about *The Art of War*, the more I realized that the old general who had written it had understood the pain of war, something I was only beginning to grasp.

"I like that approach," Atal said, nodding.

That was good. While he took care of the field, I needed to get back, to begin producing. We needed far more steel than we had, far more than I alone could make. We needed concrete for walls, mortar, and stone. We needed weapons like ballistae, which would give even a magic-user pause, and we needed all of them yesterday. I would also have to delve deeper into creating magical items. I could almost taste it, almost feel the pieces clicking together for a true magical weapon, a formidable tool that might be enough to win this war.

CHAPTER 27

WEAPONS OF WOOD AND IRON

Chien grunted as we pulled the last of the ropes taut and readied ourselves to test this machine. Next, a small bolt was brought to the fore, and we established a shield in front of us, something learned from previous mistakes.

"If this one explodes, we need to move on," the boy said. I was debating the same course of action myself, as this had taken far longer than I'd have liked.

A ballista was something akin to a giant crossbow, save a few things. Mainly, it didn't require an actual bow. Instead, it functioned on a completely different set of principles for power generation. The 'bow' was composed of straight pieces of wood, held by a form of rope spring. The tight ropes generated enormous power, enough to toss the little javelins much further than even most spells could go. This was what we were after—a weapon usable by normal elves to fight spellcasters and monsters. It would do that magnificently. Sadly, that power didn't always go where we were aiming to direct it.

The first ballista had exploded, sending chunks onto Chien and me, which had sent us both scrambling to find a healer. The second one just ripped itself apart; a nice change. The third one though, I had high hopes for. So I pulled the rope holding the line back and watched.

The bolt shattered, and I sighed. I really should have expected this particular problem—too much energy entering it at one time was just a little more than the spar of wood could take.

"Boss, are you sure this is worth it?" my assistant asked. "I mean, we could be doing a lot of other things first."

I didn't answer. Instead, I got another piece of wood and began making a shorter, fatter dart. My running theory was that the energy going down the length of the bolt was the problem. I didn't bother putting a tip on the thing as it was only for testing, but hopefully it wouldn't need one.

Once more the siege engine was reset, loaded, and aimed. This time the bolt fired true, rushing forward like a strike of lightning from the sky and slamming into a nearby tree. The tree still stood, but where the dart had struck, a massive chunk of wood had ripped away, exposing the inner bark and meat of the green giant. As for the projectile itself, it shattered like glass, sending fragments everywhere.

"That is why it is worth it," I said, pointing at the tree hundreds of feet away. There were a few magically enhanced spear-men that might have managed that throw, but it wouldn't have been an easy feat.

"It's probably still going to break and hurt people. We'll need to have someone oversee the construction and testing," Chien observed.

"Of course," I wanted to smile. The boy had learned well. He sounded a lot like me, like he was ready for the next phase of his apprenticeship.

Over the years, Chien had gotten better and better at managing the projects I gave him. He didn't even flinch at strange ideas and new ways of doing things, instead going through the same steps over and over again. He knew how to test, to observe, to look for risks and problems, and how to go about solving them. It honestly made me proud, seeing where he'd come from.

That wasn't to say that Chien had lost his sassiness, or the slight impropriety that was always present. No, he still made jokes, chased skirts, and generally acted like a jokester. Now, though, there was more, something deeper. He was growing up, really getting there.

"What?" he asked as he saw me looking at him.

"Back in my village we had a tradition, for when a boy became a man. About time for you, isn't it?" He already looked tall enough, and with how he acted, maybe he was mature enough.

"We don't do stuff like that in Atal . . ." he began.

"Perhaps," I said. I'd have to talk to someone else. Maybe when Ian came back, he'd know, even if he didn't really like the kid.

"On another note," Chien said, quickly changing the subject, "the coppersmiths you called for should be at the house soon, shouldn't they? Best not to keep them waiting." I smiled. It was clear what he was doing, but he wasn't wrong.

An hour or two after we got back, the first people began to arrive. I'd not stopped working during the interim, of course, pumping out piece after piece for our refined ballista design, along with a few steel-tipped darts. There was no reason to wait if we could get this done, and it wasn't like we had a lot of time anyway.

In all, five smiths joined me in my shop. None of them were as good as I was yet, but all of them worked metal, a rare skill right now.

"So, what did you bring us here for?" one asked. I recognized him as the man who'd once sold me poor quality copper. Sadly, he was one of the better men at working the metal.

"Today, I am going to teach you how to make iron. It's laborious and time consuming, but we need more than we currently have, and I can't make all of the supplies on my own. You lot are the men already working metal, and so we'll have to go over the differences and processes that you'll need to know."

"What's wrong with copper?" one of them asked.

"Nothing at all, but we don't have enough of it, and iron is everywhere. Iron is also harder, stronger and, in most cases, better than copper for weapons and armor. Maybe you've heard, maybe not, but there are enemies encroaching on Atal's lands, making their way toward us and destroying everything in their path. We need to defeat them, and we'll need every weapon we can make to do it."

"Maybe Atal can negotiate . . ." another started, but stopped as soon as I began shaking my head.

"They're killing kids, using them as soldiers in ways that will kill them. Atal seems to be done talking. We will fight, and we will win, because if we don't, we die, or our children die, or other loved ones die. Those are the stakes."

"So no pressure," Chien chimed in.

My statement caused all of their faces to go grim, understanding the implications of such a series of actions. Elves loved their young, cherished them. Children were such a blessing because they were so rare, nobody got tired of them, or disliked them like back on Earth. Instead, they were viewed as the greatest thing around, and to threaten them was an unbelievably grievous crime.

So we began, starting with how to separate iron ore from the sands of the beach and how to pull together from grains one of the few things that would really aid us in this war. Soldiers would fight, builders would shore our defenses, and we, we would make the weapons needed to throw the enemy down and make them regret ever coming to these lands.

CHAPTER 28

PLAN

The rains began. It was expected, anticipated, and completely normal for this land. It seemed that the world was weeping as the sky turned gray and water fell, sheet after sheet. It also meant that construction on a large project needed to take a backseat as we continued to reinforce our weapons and armor. In my home, and in so many other workshops throughout the city, metal was being shaped into weapons and armor. I left Chien in charge as I left the house, heading down the street to my meeting with Atal and his people.

Being known by sight at the palace was becoming weirder and weirder. I was getting respect, even though I was still basically a child compared to most. I was being listened to and invited to meetings. I wasn't sure how to handle it quite yet, but I was doing the best I could.

Today there were several battle mages here, and one of them looked at me. "Justin, I've a request from some of us," he said.

"What's that?" I replied. It wasn't usual that they wanted something from me. But normally, it was someone in charge of defenses, and soldiers, who asked.

"A few days ago the ancestor was telling me about the battle the two of you fought against these destroyers and their leader."

"Yes?" I nodded.

"During that time you managed to stop the scream attack from one of their more powerful people?" he said, and I could see several of his fellows now leaning closer too.

"Yes," I agreed.

"If it isn't too much of me to ask, the description of how you did so from the ancestor made little sense. Could you explain it to me, please? Such a thing might be highly useful."

There was a lot of politeness in his voice, forms of speech and inflection that almost indicated he was speaking to an elder or another high-ranking elf. I was taken aback, and then I began to think about it. Atal was placing a lot of trust in me, allowing me into places I shouldn't normally be, and telling me state secrets. It might be very true that I now ranked closer to an elder than anything else in the city right now, even if the city itself didn't use that designation.

I also wasn't under any obligation to answer him. Had it been Atal, I would have needed to, because he was a leader at war, but when it came to magic, there were some things that were private. Anyone could decide to keep most of their practices private, their insights and knowledge only given to those they trusted. Even Atal's granddaughter could have decided that I was unworthy and thrown me out, had she really wanted to. Atal had probably given her an incentive of some kind so she would teach me the things she had.

The room was silent as I considered answering his question. Even Atal was watching, not nervously, but as if he were judging my reaction, seeing what I would do. I had skin in this game, though, and wouldn't be denied a chance at seeing the man who'd killed so many of my people gone.

"I don't mind telling you that, and a few more things, but some things are too dangerous to explain. For a shield, though, this will be helpful." I then went on to give a basic explanation of how to block sound, though I didn't go too deeply into why it would work. Here I would be telling them the how, not the why, for the why might well lead to other things being discovered, which I wasn't ready to make public yet.

For a few moments, I had the floor before it returned to Atal, who looked pleased that I was sharing the info. After all, if I could protect him from a similar power to that which our enemy's leader used, then perhaps there would be more use for it in the future.

We moved on to the state of reinforcement on the villages and city itself. This was an important area, since without some form of protection, it was likely that we'd be overrun. The towers had been a success, allowing us to respond to several attacks in the last weeks, but it wasn't enough.

"We need a way to destroy them when the rains stop," Atal said, rubbing his chin.

"Weaken them now," I suggested, which is something I'd already brought up.

"Moving enough people through the rains will be troublesome, and attacking their holdings even more so," one of the other advisors said, and was the prevailing opinion.

"We don't need to attack them. We need to make them waste effort." It had taken some time, but I felt this was the best way to put it.

"Why?" Atal questioned once more.

"Their soldiers' magic is burning, and the brighter they burn, the faster they fall to ashes. We don't have to win a fight. We don't even have to fight, but making them around, making them work, will speed up their deaths."

"They are children; they are our children!" the advisor objected, seeming enraged that I would desire the deaths.

Atal's granddaughter Jina was here, the one who'd taught me about magical materials and potions, but most of the time her expertise was not needed, so she seldom spoke at these meetings. If she had an opinion one way or another on any issues, it was unknown to me, but now she stood up and spoke up.

"Those children will die either way, and there is nothing we can do about it. Is it crueler to extend their lives? Do we let them rampage and destroy even more? Or do we instead seek to kill them and spare others? I think the answer should be obvious." Having said her piece, Jina sat back down.

The room was silent. Jina was the expert on potions, the undisputed master as far as those present were concerned. She was the one who made them, and the one who made many of the inks and agents from magical plants and the like, and if she said the children were doomed, the only other person who might know different was Atal, who remained silent.

"If we can save them, we should, but unless someone manages to free their families, I don't see them returning to our side of the fight," I said.

"Then we put together a group to do as you suggested," Atal declared.

"I'll go," I offered immediately.

"No, you are needed here. If you die, we lose a good source of weapons, one we cannot spare."

With a few more words and gestures, leaders for the effort were designated. At the very least, I would see to it that they'd be as well-equipped as I could manage. If it came to a fight, they could have at least that much.

CHAPTER 29

UNTIL YOU CAN'T ANYMORE

The sky poured out upon us. It wasn't called the rainy season for nothing, and this time at least it was living up to its name. Days had passed since I'd seen the sun, but still there was work to do. As I lifted my hand, rocks moved into place, the keystone of the new gate for the city settling into place.

Atal had taken some of my suggestions to heart about increasing the city's defenses, and this was the result. We couldn't rebuild the entire wall too quickly, but the gates could be reconstructed and reinforced fairly easily. Truthfully, we probably could repair the wall, but the time simply wouldn't be worth the investment right now.

The new gates were massive—stone, and vaguely medieval—with me having added a few touches here and there based on what I could remember. It had been the weakest point, and would probably be the location of any attack, but now it might well be the hardest part to breech.

On Earth, just moving the stone and materials needed would have taken years, but with the amount of workers we had, we could brute force it. Magic also helped. Even if we could brute force some solutions, elves who could just float things where they needed to go weren't to be scoffed at.

After a few final checks, I headed home, returning to my weapons once more. Now there were a number of things in my basement that would give people pause. Perhaps one or two could even hurt Atal, if needed, and all heavily sealed in steel and stone. I slipped past these, moving to where I kept my magical crystals—today's work.

I'd thought about guns, at least cannons, but there were issues. All the chemistry I knew, all that I'd taken in school when I was a human, hadn't told me how to make saltpeter from scratch, nor nitrocellulose, and I didn't know how to even cast something like a cannon. If those went wrong, I wouldn't have a weapon to fire at my enemies, but rather a bomb near my friends. Not an appealing idea.

Biological weapons were basically a nonstarter too. Someone like my mother could have probably managed it, if they knew what they were doing, but I was no virologist, and it would be a double-edged sword either way.

Chemical weapons. Those I'd actually had a bit of success with. The most dangerous thing currently in my lab was a small sealed steel amphora of what I was fairly sure was chlorine trifluoride. It was something I'd remembered hearing about, and with a lot of effort had managed to make through magic. That process was iffy at best, slow, and incredibly dangerous. For my labors I'd made something the size of a grenade that would absolutely ruin somebody's day, and I could make more, but I worried about the danger of even storing the stuff. It was a nasty, nasty chemical.

Leaving behind the war-crime section of my basement, I moved to where the magic happened, literally. I'd been experimenting for some time on the magical crystals, and today I'd be trying once more for a new one. Producing and honing light had gone well enough, and now that I was satisfied I could make crystals, and my magic reserve had grown enough for me not to pass out doing it, I was onto a new one, force. We needed something with a good amount of oomph to take on some of these new enemies, and this might just be the thing.

If I could find a way to project pure force, that in itself would be a weapon of choice. I sort of doubted it would have the visual effect of fire, but those were the two spells I used most, so we'd be working with them. And if I could get it to work well, I might be able to do great damage with it.

My current issue was that if I just made force, it tried to go somewhere. That meant that not only did I need to make one crystal, but I'd probably also end up making two at once. I needed both directional force and whatever I was going to use to oppose it, be it a shield or an opposing force. Eventually I'd need to manage all of this into something usable, but for now getting the first step completed would be enough.

In my head, I saw a day where one of my people could sit before a screen and key in directions for the magic they wanted, and then let it fly. Simple scripts if and when I could get these tiny crystals to form outputs in the ways I wanted. Perhaps that would be dangerous though, and making many of these items would be impossible for most casters. Considerations for later, because I didn't even have a proper logic gate yet. For now I needed something that could do anything, something that could just use power well.

Hours later, I stumbled from my lab, drenched in sweat and exhausted. The mana costs were too great. Maybe if I could miniaturize? But how? I didn't even know what I was doing properly, much less how to control it better. Even with my growing reserve of magic, I'd not managed to form a crystal that I could detect. It never reached the point where it snapped into place.

Ida was in the kitchen when I arrived, working. From her stance I could tell something was bothering her. That seemed odd.

"Something wrong?" I asked curiously.

"I keep hearing more and more about these invaders," she confided, head low. "What if they get here?"

"Maybe they will," I answered, which didn't seem to comfort her at all. "Maybe they won't. What we can do right now is see to it that we're as ready as we can be for whatever comes. Though honestly, I never feel like I am properly ready for anything."

"I'm afraid."

"That's fairly normal. If you weren't, I'd be more surprised. They're killing and destroying their way across our lands."

"No, I'm afraid they'll take me, like I was before. You don't know what it's like, not having any control, knowing that you can die and nobody will care, powerless to do anything."

"You're right," I admitted. "Atal and his people scare me senseless, and he *likes* me. I can't possibly imagine what that's like. You're free to tell me, if you want, or not, but there's one thing I know. Being scared right now won't help. We need to act, be ready, and fear paralyzes."

"Not sure what I'm doing helps anyway," she griped, still in the dumps.

"Today it doesn't. Tomorrow it won't either, but a month from now? A year? Ten years? It really could. We don't know what will come or when, and we don't know if or when this conflict will end. If we have to be ready for fighting a decade in the future, I want to be the best prepared. What you're making will aid in making armor, protection for the soldiers."

"You don't have to lie to me, you know?" she teased.

"I'm not. I feel inadequate all the time, like I'm not good enough, like it should be someone else. You know what? That's true too. There are certainly people smarter, more clever, and stronger than me. Here's the thing though—I'm the one who's here, and so are you. You could go, you could leave, veer from this path and try to hide, but you aren't. Showing up is the first step, one so many never take."

She smiled. "So just keep showing up then?"

"Until you can't anymore," I nodded.

CHAPTER 30

OUT ONCE MORE

I looked down at the vague outline of my project, nowhere near done but showing the first signs of true structure. It had taken the entire rainy season, and even now it was looking very rough, but this was my weapon. Well, it would be my weapon when it was finally finished. Currently, it was just a number of small magical crystals held together by thin connecting strands.

My creation would be a hammer. I used such an instrument the most, and I liked the symbolism—the builder of civilization destroying the barbarians at the gate—so I was going with it, and when it was complete, it would pack one hell of a punch. The many individual crystals making this artifact up would all force energy in directed paths, both forward with the head, and upward away from whoever was swinging it. If I'd done all of my work correctly, it would look normal, if fancy, until the moment it struck. Upon landing, the amount of energy released should be enough to shatter stone walls—not everything I hoped for, but a start.

Control, of course, was still all manual. Surely there had to be a solution, a way to make this work with inputs, but I didn't have it yet, and I didn't have a ton of time to figure it out. For now it would do one thing and one thing only, and I hoped it could do it well enough. Maybe if I used it at just the right time, it would be enough.

All of that would sadly have to wait, for I had other projects to oversee. The nearby villages needed to be fortified, and even if the people working with me weren't fools, there were parts of the fortification that I wanted to oversee myself. Atal hadn't liked it, but with his people pushing back the enemy over the previous season, and the fact that I wasn't going far, he accepted in the end. The fact that I'd tossed most of my metalworking duties at others helped too. Now I was only working on select projects rather than the day-to-day grind of making weapons and armor.

I returned upstairs once more, gathering the last of my supplies. Isha was fussing about. This world didn't have marriage ceremonies in the same vein as Earth, but they did exist. Much like ceremonies for becoming an adult, they simply represented a shift, a change in perspective that others could see and attest to, and they varied. The only real similarity was that we had to state our intent before others. It was all rather like the contract we'd had as children, but far more serious.

"I don't like you going out there," Isha said, pouting at me.

"Been hearing that a lot lately," I answered, pulling her close. Officially married or not, we were basically already there.

"Seems like perhaps you should listen to it then."

"Isha, I'll be nearby, with guards, and this needs to happen. You know that." I kissed the top of her head, only for her to pull away.

"Someone else can do it."

"True, but nobody else can do it as well. Even Chien can't, and he's almost as good as I am nowadays." That was the truth, as the lad's magic might be well behind mine, but his ability to understand and work with designs was improving by the day.

"Fine," she said with a frown.

Before long, I bid her and the others of the house goodbye and met up with Ian. He'd be joining me for this, though he wasn't in charge of it all. Frankly, I think the powers that be knew I got along with him better than the average guard, and that's why they sent him along.

"Ready?" I asked my friend as we walked out of the gates.

"Following you around will be better than what I was doing last season," he said with a smile and a shrug.

"How'd things go?" I inquired.

"Badly, but we did it. The leaders had us tracking down where they were coming over the mountains and start taking them down one by one. These Westers are a mess."

"Westers?"

"Needed something to call them. They don't have cities, or really even villages, so Westers it is; they're from the west, after all," he explained.

"What do they call themselves?" I asked.

"The True People."

I didn't bother to disguise my displeasure with that.

"What do they call us then? The False People?"

"No, they just call us enemies from what I can tell. Honestly I'm not all that impressed with them. Their weapons are poor, and while they're pretty aggressive, they don't really build anything so far as I can tell—no houses, no walls, nothing." He was already starting down the path nearly all people did during war—dehumanizing the enemy, or in this case de-elvenizing them.

The trip to the first of the villages we were beefing up didn't even take a day. As I looked around, I realized that I'd been to this village before. This was the place I'd stopped when I first moved to Atal. We didn't waste any time when we got there. The magic users quickly began assembling walls. I'd be seeing to the gatehouse and ballista emplacements myself.

Rocks were being pulled out, cut to shape, and assembled one by one; it wasn't fast, but it would be sturdy. We'd even brought a small amount of cement along for the process. I would've preferred to use more of the material, but without a good source of limestone, we could only make it from shells or coral.

At the end of a hard day's work, I sat atop the section of wall I'd completed with Ian, sipping a basic berry wine from a waterskin. It turned out alcohol had predated agriculture in this world, even though few bothered with it.

"I saw one of those kids," he admitted after a long drink. "One of the ones they poisoned. I watched him die."

"I'm sorry to hear that. It's horrible what they're doing to them."

"He was hovering in the air, throwing stuff at us one moment, and the next . . . The boy wasn't more than twelve, couldn't have been, and he just ripped apart. One of the fire users with us said it was the power, that the unnatural nature of it killed him." Ian stared off into the distance, lost in his memories. "I've seen lots of people die, Justin, from monsters and accidents, even a few killed by criminals, or Atal when he's done with said criminals, but nothing like that. The screaming, sometimes I hear it in my sleep."

"We're going to win this, and when we do, those responsible will know pain and fear," I told him.

"Then maybe we take their kids and . . ."

"No." I knew he was in pain and that he'd probably never harm a child if it came to it, but that was a line of thought that didn't even bear speaking aloud.

"What?" He turned to me with hard eyes.

"We will not become monsters; there's no end to it. Justice, yes, but revenge against the innocent? We cannot go down that path."

For a moment I wasn't sure what he was thinking but then saw his eyes soften. "You're right," he said. "We can be better than them. The adults, though, the ones doing this."

"Oh we're going to kill the shit out of them," I agreed.

"Kill the . . ." then he snorted. "You say the weirdest things, Justin." He passed me the wine, shaking his head.

CHAPTER 31

✧

ATOP A HILL

Elves weren't dumb. They were uneducated on a lot of things and uncaring about a large number of matters that people from the 'modern' world were concerned about, but not dumb. If they knew there was an army coming, they prepared as best they could. This made it a lot easier for me to do my job; people who were accepting of what they needed to do and who were willing to get to work were a lot easier to deal with. Walls were prepped before I arrived, and workers were ready to listen when I told them what I needed.

"All right, everyone, once you're here and it's aimed at the target, you slap it like so." I did just that on the trigger that I'd cobbled together, launching the practice bolt with a *whoosh* before it slammed into a tree. "Let's get some practice."

I stepped back and let them have at it, keeping watch as one by one they came up to work the contraption. As I stood there watching the villagers, I was approached by the local elder. She'd also been keenly observing those chosen to operate the ballista.

"That is an interesting machine," she said, peering at the weapon as it tossed another lance at a dead tree.

"Thank you, Elder," I responded with a small nod.

"Would it be difficult to build them ourselves? Make more for what is coming?"

I'd already considered that particular question myself. "I doubt it, but you are welcome to try. The most difficult parts to make will be the metal ones. Without enough material or the know-how, you're unlikely to manage it. Most things like wood and rope just cannot take the power needed in the same way."

"There are some materials from monsters that might," she retorted, seeing what I thought of that.

"Perhaps, perhaps not. I've not had access to many, but I know of none that would do it."

"What about the spears?"

"You can and should make some of those," I agreed. "While you may not be able to make any as good as the metal-tipped ones, you'll need extras for practice, and even after that, a wooden one will still hit hard enough to do real damage."

The machines themselves weren't brought in fully built. Wood was everywhere, so we gathered as much as we needed on site for each ballista, assembling them from the pieces that had been made in the capital and handed them over. Mostly, there were metal parts and ropes, an idea I'd taken from armies of the past.

Days passed and we worked our way outward. The path wasn't an exact spiral—with the lack of maps, it was hard to tell exactly what shape it was—but we were slowly working our way toward the edge of the inner villages. Those villages farther away from Atal would need to deal with things themselves, but the ones closest would be fortified for now.

As we neared the end of our trip, I briefly wondered what all this would do in the end. Would it be enough? Would we manage to destroy them all, or would we fall? There was a real chance that they'd have too many mages and would simply overwhelm us in the end.

We crested a hill and something felt . . . off. It took me a few seconds to realize what it was, and then it hit me. The woods had gone silent. The bugs, the birds, the little critters here and there, had all frozen.

The instant I realized it, I threw up shields around us, and not a second too soon. They'd barely made it into place before several spells splashed against them, angry purple magic licking at the barriers.

Our group numbered only about ten for this leg of the journey, but all of us moved quickly. Spears were pointed outward, and those with magic began charging their own abilities. From far behind us, I heard someone yell as if an attack had landed true, but we held.

I needed to act quickly, strike decisively, because this was a different kind of magic. With the way they moved, the odd colors, it looked more like my mother's magic than mine. I could mostly affect the physical world, but others worked with organic compounds and living things. Such magics could be deadly and fast.

Opening with two bolts of flame, I launched my projectiles, hoping to find the enemies, or at least limit their angles of attack.

"Get down!" Ian yelled, pulling me backward as a spell hurled itself in my direction.

At first I hadn't worried about it, but where it hit the shield I could see it cracking, the magics competing to hold.

"We need cover!" I responded, looking around.

There was nothing though. The enemy had chosen this spot well. All around us were trees, easy protection for them. We didn't have cover though? There had been rocks or something else to hide behind, but they had been moved. There were small indents in the ground that I'd missed before.

I saw Ian throw a spear, only to have it barely scrape his target. As he did so, we lost two people, purple orbs striking them and spreading a black necrosis across their skin.

"In the center," I heard an enemy yell.

Naturally, I was in the center. The soldiers were here supposed to be guarding me.

One of my shields shattered and I ducked, only for the offending projectile to slip inches from my skin and into Ian's shoulder. He froze, like he couldn't move, almost as if he'd been tazed, and then he fell, shaking and gasping at my feet.

Quickly, the group disbanded, leaving me at the center, alone with Ian. I stood over my fallen friend, looking out and throwing all the spells I could. Could I have fled? Maybe, but not with him, not with the others, and looking around, I doubted I'd get far. No, it would be better to end it here, take as many of the bastards down with me as I could.

I'd practiced for this, not even knowing that I had. The shields got a refresh, and then I began to turn the magic in my hands. A sphere of force as opaque as I could make it, filled with fire. It grew hotter and hotter, brighter and brighter as I forced my power into it. If I could create crystals from fire magic, I could certainly wipe out some of these fools.

The enemy's attacks battered my defenses nearly all the way down before I thrust my hands forward, aiming for what looked like the largest part of their strike force.

The orb I'd launched popped like a balloon upon impact. Instead of helium, it was filled with white-hot death. It was as if a bomb had gone off on one side of the hill, filling the expanse with blinding light and searing temperatures. Trees near the explosion were knocked down. Even trees thirty feet from impact instantly found themselves aflame. Oddly, there was no screaming. They must have simply died too quickly.

Before I could form a second thought, I was struck. It didn't hurt, not in the slightest. No, it felt more like being hit with a snowball. There was a quick wave of chill and then numbness as my muscles loosened and refused to move, accompanied by a wash of confusion as everything spun.

I must have been on the ground, which was odd. I couldn't feel the ground, the rocks and sticks and grass poking into me, but I must have been. Above me stood a man, and while his face came in and out of focus, I could see rage in his eyes.

"You're lucky I was ordered to bring you back alive," he said, and then darkness took me.

CHAPTER 32

GO TO SLEEP

I came to slowly. As I snapped my eyes open to look around, I saw my captors. I wasn't their only captive; they'd taken Ian too. We were each being carried by the same man, tied and slung over his shoulder. One of the others soon realized that I was awake, even though I'd held off speaking.

"Ah, you're back with us then?" he said sweetly. "Let me introduce myself. I'm Osla, and if I'm not mistaken, you're Justin. Our leader is so very interested in speaking to you."

"How wonderful; to what do I owe the honor?" I asked, not bothering to hide my sarcasm.

"Oh now, now, I think you know," he said with a smile. "You're a very useful man."

"Capturing one with power is difficult," I said. I was already trying to think of ways I might escape.

"It is true, but that's why we brought your friend here," he replied genially. "I don't doubt that with time you might be able to slip away, but if you do, I'll peel the flesh from his bones while he screams your name."

Ah, so that was their game. After all, it had worked with the children. Why not with the adults? It did complicate things, but I still had a feeling there would be a way, when the time was right.

"Why him though?" I asked.

"Did you not think we were paying attention? You stood over your friend here while the others fell. Then again, if he's not important we can just kill him now, save everyone the trouble."

"I would rather you not," I replied. He'd called my bluff beautifully, and patted my back as if to comfort me.

"Don't worry my friend, don't worry at all. Ancient Cino really does want you around, it seems. If you prove useful, you might even find a place in our new order. It is an honor we'll be extending to only a few." It wasn't lost on me that this guy really liked to talk, and was trying to be buddy-buddy. Maybe he was an interrogator, maybe he was a recruiter. I didn't yet know for sure, but probably a bit of both.

Eventually, I was placed on my feet and made to walk. That suited me fine, as it gave me more of an idea of where we were going, not that I knew the area that well. It also allowed Osla to keep talking. If he'd been telling me anything useful, it might have served a purpose, but instead he was going on about the local plants, how food was different across the mountains, and generally safe topics. Honestly, it was a surprise he didn't bring up the weather, but that wasn't a trope here yet.

Ian took longer to come to. Unlike me, he was promptly informed that he was a hostage and quite disposable, and then he was mostly ignored. Osla even moved him to a different part of the group, both to keep me going and to keep control, no doubt.

"If you don't mind my asking, what brought this invasion on?" I inquired as the sun began to set. "I doubt you're doing it for fun."

"No," my captor said seriously. "We are not." There was a break, a short silence before he sighed. "There's a drought on the other side of those mountains, a long one. Near them it's not so bad, but further out? No rain for almost three years. People were starving, unable to find food, unable to find water."

"What about using magic?" I asked. Such spells were fairly common.

"It helps, but it's not enough. We need to move, and unfortunately, your people are in the way. It also doesn't solve the monster problem. You see, as the water got less and less, there were fewer places for monsters to go. First they congregated around the water sources that were left, and then they started fighting over them. Most of the things over there nowadays are horrors, able to raze an unprepared village. As even the places they've taken over dry, though, they move and try to find others, destroying everything in their way." His eyes were far off, thinking about where he'd come from.

It made sense. Greed alone could have been the motivator, but with added need? I can't say that invading was the wrong choice, but that wasn't my main problem with it.

"But the children; you're killing them. You know that, right?"

Osla had a pained look, a tired look. "I do, and I'm sorry for it. Sadly, we don't have enough people to do it without them, or we would. In the end though, your children are less important to me than ours."

We didn't get much further. They found a cave where we could all settle down. Ian and I were, of course, near the rear, while the others took positions closer in to watch us. They gave us some food and water, then set up a guard shift.

"How'd you find us, by the way?" I asked over dinner.

Osla snorted. "Let's just say some of the folk around here have seen where things are going, and they know which side they want to be on when it's all done." I'd suspected as much, but confirmation was good. "No, I won't tell you who, and no, you won't be seeing any of them, just in case you get any ideas." That also solved some of my worries, letting me make more immediate plans.

"How are you even doing it?" asked Ian from beside me, clearly angry. "I may not know much, but I know what you're doing to the kids isn't easy."

Osla sneered at him, then steadied his face. "To tell the truth, I'm not entirely sure. The ancient's new whore told him about it, some kind of plant or something. She hates you lot, sold you out. One day it'll come back to get her, I'm sure. Hah, she even asked that we execute some guy named Elian; got her exiled or something according to her." I carefully schooled my face; it wasn't unexpected, but I didn't want to give anything away.

"And you think he'll give her what she wants?" I answered.

"Oh yes, Cino's good on his word, takes pride in it. Of course I know he also hates traitors, so as soon as she's had her revenge, he'll probably pour boiling sap down her throat. I mean, how many girls has he had over the years? She's nothing special. Stick around and you'll almost certainly get to see. Bit of revenge for what she did to you guys, right?" There was the wicked smile again, the monster underneath the facade of civility.

He left us to think after that, everyone getting ready for sleep. Ian and I laid back as I set things into motion, an idea I'd been rolling around since we arrived at the cave.

When most of the crew, except the guard and us, had settled down, I began. First, I set up a pair of barriers, one over the cave entrance and one over me and Ian. They didn't need to be strong, but they did need to stop air, so it was a weird balancing act. I also didn't want them visible—something that probably wouldn't have been possible in proper daylight, but there was only the small light the guard made to keep everything in sight, and it wasn't bright enough to see them.

Getting a proper air mixture in the bubble around Ian and me was a bit of a guessing game. I knew that I needed about twenty percent oxygen, and began to carefully manage that, and then I began to alter the mix around our hosts.

I could visualize nitrogen molecules, two atoms with triple bonds, and carbon monoxide as well with ease; it was much the same, but with different atoms. If I could visualize it, I could make it, so make it I did. It took time, and I feared what I was doing. I knew the results. This wasn't like a battle; it just felt different. I also knew what would happen if I didn't do it, and that steeled my resolve.

Without carbon dioxide building up in their blood, there was no alert, no sense of doom. Doom was coming, though, a silent, sure one, without screams, or pain, or glory—just death taking their breath without them even realizing it.

The guard didn't seem to realize what was going on but clearly knew he was sleepy. He stood briefly, splashing water on his face and smacking it before yawning and sitting back down. A few minutes later, the light he was maintaining went out as he slipped into sleep.

"Justin," Ian whispered, nodding. "We need . . ."

"Quiet, just wait," I answered in the same hushed voice. "Don't do anything." I really didn't want them waking up.

I made my own light while we sat there, time ticking by until one by one the sound of snoring stopped. Even then I gave it more time, because we'd likely only get once chance at this. Once the only sound we heard was our breathing, Ian turned back to me.

"Are they?" he asked.

"Yes, but we'll need to make sure of it," I answered, floating over one of their knives.

"But how?" he asked. "You . . . They're just dead?" He looked at me, alarm on his face.

"It's not something I like, or that I want to explain. Let's just finish this." With that, I used my magic to force the blade into one of their chests, not getting a reaction.

CHAPTER 33

✦

THE PATH HOME

We left the cave as the sun rose and quickly began our travel home; it was sure to be a difficult trip. It was just me and Ian, and he was scared of me. He didn't say it at first; instead just quick, nervous glances here and there.

Even if I spent most of my time indoors and within the city, I was still well versed in navigation. There were tricks to it, things to look out for, ways to keep oneself from getting lost or turned around. Direction was important, and without practice, someone might not even realize they had been walking in circles for days. Part of the reason behind this was that elves, much like humans, favored one side of their body over the other, veering their steps more to the favored side. More importantly though was the fact that under the cover of trees the sun wasn't always visible, and in the afternoon it might be difficult to tell which direction was which.

Words were few as we moved through the morning light, picking our way along game trails and the occasional small creek. It was easier to move fast this way, along the paths that weren't roads rather than through proper jungle, which could be a hard place to run at the best of times. As we stopped to rest around lunchtime, Ian turned to me.

"So, do you have a plan?" he asked.

"Yes, get back to Atal, and avoid any of the villages while we do so." It wasn't a complicated plan, but simple plans had a better chance of success in my experience.

"You don't think they were bluffing about traitors then?"

"No," I answered. "Atal is terrifying to me, and he likes me. Even if he doesn't mean to be, even if he's trying to be nice, he comes off as scary. It doesn't surprise me in the least that a few would welcome someone else."

"Almost sounds like you'd think of joining them," he said.

"They're killing children, Ian. They already killed my village. From what Isha told me, it was their leader, Cino, who ordered it and carried it out. It's no secret I didn't love the elder there, but I didn't want her dead!" I snapped.

"Sorry," he said, making a placating gesture. "I meant no offense. On the subject of killing, though, what happened back there?"

"I suffocated them," I answered.

"Justin, I've seen people suffocated before, and strangled, and stabbed. They just . . . fell asleep. I've never seen anything like that. How?"

I looked at him for a few moments. How did I want to explain this? Did I want to explain it at all? I didn't have to; it was one of my spells, and those were private. There also wasn't any theory at all about different gases here. Sure, people knew that smoke was a thing, and that bad smells happened, but the idea that there were a lot of different components to air that could change it like I had? Nobody knew of anything even mildly similar to that.

Even if I did tell him, and in a way that he could understand, would it give others a new tool against me? It might, and it would be hard to counter. Of course, I was only capable of what I'd done because I knew way more about molecular structures than they did, not something I was willing to part with, or could explain at all.

"There are many kinds of air," I finally answered. "It is difficult to explain, but some of them are not so good for you. Like a cave filled with smoke. You couldn't breathe that, right?"

"I guess not," he said. "But there was no smoke, no smell. They didn't even look like they noticed."

"Yes, that's the trick to it. It's complicated, Ian, but that's how I did it—bad air."

It was an answer that wasn't really an answer. What was 'bad air' to him? He wouldn't know anything useful from what I'd told him. Certainly people here died of suffocation in caves and whatnot sometimes, and if you could use that as a weapon, it would indeed be a powerful one. Well, maybe not, seeing as it could only be used under a few circumstances. He didn't need to know that though.

Ian shook his head. "You know, Justin, some days I feel worthless next to you. I sometimes think about when we first met. You were barely a man, wandering somewhere you didn't quite understand. Now look at you, sought by ancients and put in charge of these projects, and I can't do anything worthwhile; I don't even have real strength."

I looked away. Sure, it was possible to give him some line, some sappy story about how he was really useful, but the honest truth was that he wasn't particularly strong, nor smart. Ian didn't have any outstanding talents, and even if he worked hard, he'd not chosen a field where he could ever truly be an outstanding person, unless he had magic, of course.

"You're an all-right guy. My aunt likes you well enough at least." It wasn't much, but it was the best I could come up with on the spot.

He gave me a hesitant look. "I, uh, didn't mean to tread on any . . ."

"What? I don't care. If she's happy, I'll be happy for her." It was clear that the only reason he'd not made a serious move was that he worried about how I'd react, but honestly I didn't care.

"Seriously? What about, well, your uncle or whatever."

"Never had one as far as I know. Anyway, why should I care? Atie's a big girl; she can make her own decisions."

"Ah, I wasn't expecting you to be okay with that, Justin," he admitted.

"Yeah, go nuts. Of course, if you hurt her, they'll never find your body." I gave him a small smile, only to see him pale in response.

It didn't occur to me until much later how potent of a threat that was. Had he ever been exposed to that particular part of my society? Not really. I was also a terror compared to most of the people in my age group. With money, magic, and political power backing me, I could probably kill him with ease and nobody would even look.

Shortly after that, the conversation died. With nothing else to say, we readied the gear we had either retained or taken when leaving the dead kidnappers behind and set back off. Neither of us wanted to be here. Nor did we want to risk getting attacked by enemy elves or the many beasts that roamed this land.

The only solution to our problem would be to get home and back to those we loved. It was also important that we quickly inform Atal that there were betrayers amongst our people who needed to be dealt with quickly. Enemies like that would be a major obstacle to victory in this war. After all the crimes of the Westers, I felt no pity for whoever Atal might target among those who betrayed us.

CHAPTER 34

JOURNEY WITH IAN

We walked for days. Unable to use the main routes or trust that the nearby villages were on our side, we took much longer to cover ground. We weren't even completely sure where we were, our only guides being the sky and the way the land moved. It would be enough; it had to be enough.

Three nights in, I lay in a field beside my companion, looking up at the clear night sky. It amazed me how pristine it was, the wide bands of blues and yellows stretching from one end of my vision to the other. As I lay there, I had a thought and sat up.

"You thought of something," Ian commented, chuckling to himself.

"Yes, the stars. Do they stay the same over time?" I asked.

"Hmm? No, they migrate like the birds, coming round and round by the year. Didn't you know that?"

"No, never really paid much attention to them. Do they always come back to the same place?" I inquired further.

"Of course."

"So, could we use them to find our way?" I said excitedly.

"Justin, I've already been doing that. Normally you don't need them to navigate, but going far, like warriors sometimes do, you need to know a bit." Now he actually laughed. "Sorry, but you were beaten to that discovery long ago."

"Could you show me?"

Ian looked almost taken aback. "You know, some days I forget how young you are. Come here then, friend, and I'll teach you what you should've known long ago."

I made a face, hoping he couldn't read my embarrassment. Really I should have paid more attention to this, but I just hadn't. Sure, I knew a few things, but nothing about navigation; it just hadn't occurred to me. It was also great to find that there was something others had thought of first in this world.

If I remembered correctly, stargazing was one of the first things any human society had done. The night sky was just there every night, clearly painted with something too beautiful for anyone to really ignore for long. Perhaps in smaller villages it was mostly ignored, but in large cities where people had to travel for weeks or months in potentially untamed wilds? No, it was clear why it was known.

In the end, though, the information I got was pretty general—the way the galactic disc pointed during certain times of the year, and a few of the more visible constellations for this time of year and what they could mean based on what season it was. Ian's knowledge was general, not that of an expert. Maybe there were people who were experts, maybe not. I just didn't know.

If I could math out a basic system for timekeeping and angles, we could probably get a rough estimate of things. On the other hand, I didn't need that right now, nor would we in the foreseeable future. One day perhaps, we'd need something like this to make sailing possible. For the moment, it was just one more thing to add to the list, and that list was already long enough.

Over the next few days, Ian and I talked about our techniques for hunting and navigation. They were similar. Where plants were concerned, though, some of the ones we encountered on our trek I'd never seen. My home had been further inland, whereas Ian came from a coastal area, so some of the vegetation further inland was novel to him.

"I can't believe you've never seen these," I said as I picked a few berries.

"Eh, we had meat and weren't really looking for something to snack on," he explained. "The few times I went out, we mostly stuck to what we already knew, and most of the soldiers are from Atal too."

Honestly, that particular bush, with its deep purple fruit, had been a rare find. I'd seen no others like it on this trip. Maybe a bird had been migrating, or perhaps it had washed out in a flood or something. There weren't even any others nearby. I knew because I looked.

After a couple more days, we had a visitor. I heard it before I saw it, the distinctive cawing a dead giveaway. Following our ears through thickets and a few briars, we soon found the source.

On a rock, in the middle of a small pond sat a seabird, a simple, solitary seabird eating a fish. It was something you could see any day near the docks of Atal, or along the coast. These creatures were little better than rats with wings, making a mess everywhere. I never thought I'd be so happy to see one of the little avians.

"What a wonderful omen," Ian said. "I ate one of those once. Ever tell you that?"

"No, but I'm not surprised. Did it taste good?"

"Stringy, but not bad."

I sighed. "Maybe we'll have one another time."

We'd been surviving on berries and whatever we could eat on the go, and meat was not on the menu. We'd wanted to cook meat, but the smell of meat cooking would alert animals and other people for miles around.

We hurried our pace and went on far longer into the evening than we'd dared before. Running through the night had been for naught. It became clear that we'd either have to use light or risk injuring ourselves. Neither of those options appealed to us, so we stopped and rested, determined to wake up as early as possible the next day.

The sun rose over crashing waves the next morning. Ian and I had both woken up in the pre-dawn light and agreed without words to continue. We'd made it just in time to see the first beams streak above the horizon. It was a magnificent sight, if only because it told us we were almost home.

CHAPTER 35

SENTINEL

Walking alongside the beach was a refreshing change. It wasn't all good, but it did at least make navigation far, far easier. Sadly it also brought sand, a pain to walk in, a pain to be around, just generally a pain. Let us not forget that where there is sand, there are sand flies, meaning that as we made our way down the beach, we woke up in the mornings with all kinds of bites.

On the upside, we now had new and simple sources of food, like crab, shellfish, and coconuts. The last of which were, as far as I could tell, exactly the same as the ones from my previous world. All of these could be gathered with ease as we pushed forward, either by picking them off rocks and sand or with my magic, snatching the little crustaceans from where they skittered nearby. After some thought, I even managed to figure out a way to cook them with magic. That mostly involved holding them in a little kinetic box in the surf and heating the inside to boiling—mana intensive, but effective.

As even more days passed, I began to notice a change in my companion, though not one I could readily explain. People like myself—those with magic—had an aura, a sort of visual phenomenon around them. This was a constant, though with a bit of effort, I could make mine appear smaller or larger. Each aura was unique, a type of calling card. There was also at least some correlation with power; I noticed that the stronger someone was magically, the more energetic their aura tended to be. Atal's, for example, was a terrifying cloud in his general area.

However, most elves didn't really display much. There might be a little poof of magic around them whenever they used their ability, but little more. All elves I'd ever seen had at least some magical ability, and this mostly manifested as a slight distortion when using it. Ian's, though, was flashing more than normal. It was as if there was a flickering light, sending an almost marbled sheen through the air.

Normally I'd have tuned this out, but the flashing got my attention. In fact, I ignored auras most of the time unless someone was doing something with one, or unless someone had one that was oddly potent.

"Hey, are you using your strength a lot?" I finally asked, confused.

"No, why?"

"Because you're sort of flashing; never seen something like that before." I was trying to parse it, but some things just didn't add up.

"Odd, maybe we can ask someone when we get back to the city?" he suggested.

"Yeah, probably should." I didn't really like the idea of something going wrong with my friend's power. We'd already seen what could happen with the kids, and as far as I knew, anything like that was detrimental.

Jina would certainly know, if one of the older elves didn't. If it was a common, or even slightly abnormal thing, it should be known. I just had to wait and hope that it wasn't something too dangerous.

Along our route, there were clear signs of other elves nearby—footprints or pits in the sand. One morning we even got close enough to see a group of girls harvesting mussels from some rocks, but we avoided them. Neither of us knew the villages around this part of the coast, and we still had to suspect that there was a traitor somewhere who'd sold us out.

Did the hunters from those villages realize we were passing through? I didn't know, but if they did, they didn't approach us. It was likely that if someone followed our trail for even a little while, they realized we were just passing through and were nowhere near where they lived. Technically, if we got close enough, we were supposed to give our regards to the village elder, but without knowing where those villages were, it wasn't abnormal behavior to just keep walking.

The worst thing that could happen was to be mistaken as part of the enemy force. That would cause a quick and violent response. Were the villages in this part of our lands even concerned with that though? Most of the invaders had been in the mountains, slowly creeping east, not near the coast.

Eventually, we came upon a rock, jutting forth from the frothing waves. It stood like a spire in the sea—tall, lonely, and without any others in its immediate vicinity. Among the rocky and sandy coasts, the places where waves crashed upon the shore, it stood out, a sentinel.

"Wait, I know what that is," Ian said.

"Oh?"

"Yeah, it's one of the landmarks we use during training, about a day's march from the city. If we hurry, we'll eat lunch tomorrow within the walls!" he cheered. We were tired, and this was just the thing to bring our spirits up.

This landmark was visible for a mile or more in any direction, but still we rushed to pass it. Ian and I wanted to get back to our loved ones, back to our home, back to safety. We needed to alert Atal to the potential of traitors in our midst and strike back for the damage done to our unit. So close, we were so close.

The stone faded into the distance behind us, but before it was fully out of sight, I heard a slight rustling. I didn't even hesitate to put up a shield.

"You hear that?" I asked Ian.

"Yeah." He was on edge too, and carefully we picked our way toward the source of the sound.

There were a number of monsters in this world that we wouldn't want behind us. It was probably nothing too dangerous this close to civilization, but just in case, we needed to take a look. Worst case scenario, we had to retreat, something I was confident we'd be able to do, as long as we weren't caught with our metaphorical pants down. Actual pants were something I hadn't yet introduced to this world.

After another rustle we found it—a bird perched atop an odd rock. With a sigh, I lowered the shield and shook my head at my companion. I was clearly too jumpy for this right now. A good drink and a proper sleep would do me wonders.

It was for that reason that I wasn't properly prepared when the beast charged. The rock was no rock at all, but rather stony skin from something roughly the size of an alligator. In a single fluid movement, it rose and threw itself at me, large maw opening to snap at my frail body.

My instinctive dodge was fast enough to avoid getting bitten, but I was still tossed when it struck, slamming into one of the nearby trees. I briefly realized that I'd seen one of these beasts before. Then there was a crushing, agonizing sensation, which took my breath away.

I tried to pull some kind of defense around myself as it turned, glaring at me. Before the monster or I could fully angle an attack, though, something hit its side like a cannonball.

CHAPTER 36

RETURN

Agony spread from my ribs as I watched Ian tackle the monster. It clawed and he ducked, turned, and came up beside it punching. He was fast. I could follow his movements, but not well, and each strike landed with a loud *thump* as his fist impacted the stony hide of the monster.

With each punch, the aura around him sputtered to life. It pulsed like an old engine trying to turn over, again and again. It also wasn't enough, with my friend being tossed back by one of the creature's strikes. Unlike me, however, he rolled properly and came to a crouch.

Not one to be outdone, I used the moment of their separation to launch my own assault. A flurry of force missiles in arcing trajectories, all aiming for the face of the creature. The rock-pig thing tried to dodge, but I wasn't going to be letting up any time soon. Each of my arrows struck the granite hide, ripping away chunks and exposing its pink flesh underneath. My concentration was broken when I began to cough and hack. Unable to stop my diaphragm from spasming, I couldn't continue.

Ian surged forward. I'd never seen him use so much magic before. I didn't even know he could. He also didn't hesitate to take advantage of the vulnerable spots I'd left on the beast, fist slamming into flesh, instead of the hardened rock, and penetrating. The result was nothing short of fountains of blood spraying from each hole in the beast his hands had made.

I'd not bothered trying to sit up as he finished the creature, but I did reach up to lightly punch his leg when he came back to check on me. His armor had somehow held. It was a bit roughed up but still in place and covered in gore.

"Nice work," I said before coughing, a metallic taste spreading through my mouth. That wasn't good.

"Justin, we need to get you to a healer," he said, huffing.

"A day's march, and I don't think I'm marching, my friend. If you hurry, I might survive long enough for you to get back, but you'll have to leave me." I smiled. We both knew that there was very little chance of him abandoning me, but it was the best option.

"That's not happening," he replied, carefully moving to wrap his arms around me.

"Wait," I said. I did not want to be jostled, knowing all the pain that would come with it. I wrapped my body in a cocoon of force, hoping it would be enough to last until he got tired and had to sit me down. It was clear from the look on his face that there was no chance of him leaving me behind. "If you're determined, we only need to get close enough for an emergency flare."

Without words he picked me up. It still sent a wave of agony through me to be moved, but with the stability I'd managed, it wasn't nearly as bad as it could have been. Then he began to run, fast. Not bothering with the forest and the difficulty of dodging branches and vines, he headed for the beach proper, getting close enough for the wet sand to give him at least some footing as he sprinted.

"That thing shouldn't have attacked," he griped. "They're cowards, normally just pretending to be rocks. Only time I've seen one act like that is when they come up against something that's attacked them before."

I laughed, a mistake, but one that I didn't regret. "Atal used several for targets. One of them escaped, and I guess he recognized me."

"Pretty sure that was a *she*, Justin, but never mind that." The sand began to whiz by faster and faster.

"Careful, you'll wear yourself out," I chastised. "Using so much of your power already, you've got to be tired."

He blinked, then looked at me where he cradled me in his arms. "Wait, why don't I? This feels normal, almost like a light jog . . ."

Well that wasn't right. We were flying down the beach, each moment getting just a little faster. Curious, I looked at his legs, and they weren't pumping hard. He was just pushing hard, far harder than a normal person could, with each step carrying us much farther than it had any right to.

I immediately checked his aura. Rather than sputtering and flashing like it had been, it seemed to almost vibrate. If anything, it was becoming more and more solid by the moment. It was a marbled thing, like stone carved from a mountain and polished to a shine. Even as I watched, it began to settle into a firm structure, the vibrations through it seeming to put all the pieces into place.

Now I laughed in earnest, a huge guffaw. My ribs weren't amused in the least though and made me cough hard, spraying a bit of red from my mouth. Even through the pain, it was funny, and I'd been so worried.

"I have good news," I wheezed once I was able. "Your grandfather was right. Congratulations!"

"Stop laughing, you idiot, before it kills you," he snapped. "And thanks."

He ran like that for a couple of hours, and it was fast—easily two or three times faster than it would've been otherwise. However, magically empowered or not, he still had limits. As time passed, sweat began to pour off of Ian's face, his breathing beginning to struggle slightly. We were close, so close, and he refused to give up.

As he was wearing down, so was I. Keeping my own magic going for so long was hard in my state, and I was getting more and more tired by the second. Sleep, a sleep I'd likely never wake from, began to creep up on me. It felt so peaceful, so welcoming. If I just let it take me . . .

Isha's crying face flashed before my eyes, and that was enough for me to stir right as Ian stumbled.

"I need . . ." he said breathlessly, managing to put me down before he crumpled.

"Rest," I answered with a peaceful smile. "You're not alone."

Willing my magic to move, I formed a ball. One of the first spells I'd learned, one Elaya had taught me as a child, one of the first I'd even seen others use. The ball of light flew high, pulsing colors and patterns into the sky. It went up, up, over the trees, as high as I could send it, and it shone like a second sun.

There were a number of flare patterns for emergencies, and this one was simple. It told anyone looking upon it that help was needed, no immediate danger. Rather than soldiers, we needed aid, and with that flare, we might get it.

I was awake enough to see when they found us. It wasn't guards or soldiers who came to our rescue, but rather a cadre of women. From the looks of their baskets and tools it appeared they'd been out gathering. The first to see us as we lay in the sand let out a high-pitched call for the others, and soon we were surrounded.

Their leader made their way to Ian first. He had a lot more blood on him than I did, but the soldier quickly waved her in my direction. She took one look at me and began to sing, a welcoming, gentle tune the warm feeling flowing over me, lulling me into a deep sleep.

CHAPTER 37

HOSPITAL VISIT

Consciousness returned to me slowly, creeping, throbbing. It wasn't the agony of broken bones or confusion, just pain.

I opened my eyes and found myself in a room I'd been in before, but it was not expected. Along the walls were all the plants and stones I'd come to learn, the ingredients for so many potions and inks.

"Hmm, you're awake," Jina said, looking over me. "Imagine you're still hurting though."

"Ugh," I responded, not really wanting to get into it. "I see I survived."

It was good to see Jina. As Atal's granddaughter and one of the most skilled magic users in the city, I had confidence that if anything had been seriously wrong with me, I was in good hands.

"How's Ian?" I asked.

"The other boy? Oh he's fine—few scratches and bruises but nothing of note, and certainly nothing you should concern yourself with until you're doing better," she chided, poking me in the side and sending a wave of pain over me.

"Could you not do that?" I asked.

"I could, but I want to remind you to stay still. Your bones are mostly where they should be now, but it'll take time for them to be all healed up."

"Honestly, I'm surprised you couldn't just wave a hand and set it right," I said, laughing.

She looked at me for a time, then sighed. "Justin, there are limits, limits as to what can be repaired at once. The body can only take so much power in, only do so many things before it becomes dangerous. If you had just a normal broken rib, I could mend that with ease." She frowned before continuing. "On the other hand, if you come in with half of your ribs in shambles, a lung punctured and full of blood, and plenty of other things, it will take time."

"Ah, I see. Anything I can do to help?" I asked. "Other than staying still of course."

"Yes, you can eat. I'll have some food brought in to you. I'm sure that girl will be happy to hear you've woken up. Also, don't do anything strenuous or stress-inducing." The way she said the last part with a frown told me exactly what she was thinking.

She left, and soon enough Isha came to join me, bringing with her a heaping platter of food. I hadn't realized just how hungry I was until the scent of the roasted meats and tubers reached me, tickling my nose and reminding me of the food I so often ate at home. It was not all that different from what seemed to be served in Atal's palace, probably because there were only so many rare ingredients around.

"Hey there," I said with a smile.

"I told you I didn't like you going out there," she fussed, taking a spot beside me.

"But it really . . ." I didn't manage to finish as a hunk of meat was shoved into my open mouth.

"Was a bad idea? Yes, I know. You need to learn to listen, Elian, you're not unkillable, and being called here to find you pale and broken as the healers were trying to put you back together was *awful*. I thought you were dead, and when I saw you, I thought you were going to die in front of me." She continued to frown, and I wondered just how mad she was. "Also, Jina has a very poor opinion of you."

"Well, I . . ." Before I could come up with an excuse, more food was shoved into my face, gumming up the whole process.

"So, what I want to hear is that in the future you're going to listen to me and not go out when I tell you not to," she said in a huff.

"Isha, I . . ." At this point I had to grab her wrist. She seemed to know that I wasn't going to just consent to her demands and didn't want to hear it. "I'm sorry for what happened." Her shoulders fell. "But there will be times when I need to do things that you don't like, when I have to go places that will be dangerous. I want you to know that, and that I don't want to hurt you or scare you, and that I still care about you, but I can't just do nothing."

Her face went through a whole series of emotions—pain, fear, love—until she spoke again. "I am very cross with you, Elian," she finally declared.

"I love you too," I answered.

"For someone so smart, why are you so stupid?" she asked, this time offering me a bite rather than forcing it.

"Don't know," I said, shrugging. "Maybe you need to be a bit dumb to get things done sometimes."

We had time, so she ate, and I ate more; and soon enough, I finally relaxed again. She told me about what had been going on while I was gone. It wasn't anything particularly important, just little anecdotes from her life, things people had said or done while I was away, and stories about daily life. I listened, drinking it all in, never tiring of hearing about these things—the parts that made up the world that we never really paid attention to.

Eventually, she laid her head on my shoulder and we just sat there. It was peaceful, joyful, relaxing in a way that I seldom felt. Even with the pain still radiating out from my ribs, having her there brought me to a near meditative state.

All good things come to an end, though, and soon enough Jina returned. She gave us a complicated look, but not one that was disapproving. I often forgot that other people had lives and feelings, stories I didn't know, and I suspected she was no different.

"Grandfather would like to speak to you, if you're feeling up to it," she informed me.

"Of course, there's things going on that I'm sure he's got questions about, and I do too," I answered before turning to my companion. "Isha love, could you go put those away while I meet with Atal?" I said, gesturing to the dishes. "This shouldn't take too long."

Atal was an ally, but that didn't mean I wanted him anywhere near people I cared about. He liked me, wanted me on his side, but he was still dangerous, still capable of cruelty. If Isha said something he didn't like, or did something to anger him, he might hurt her, and if he did, there would be no peace between us. So I sent her away from his approaching presence—not too far, but hopefully far enough not to expose her to something I feared may cause her harm.

I also didn't want her to worry too much about the traitors we'd learned were in our midst. It wouldn't help; it would only make her more fearful. I'd be needing to add more security to our home anyway—work on keeping things safe—but there was a difference between that and the knowledge that there were several elders who were potentially trying to outright capture me.

CHAPTER 38

✧

MEETING WITH ATAL

I am glad that you have returned to me." Those were the first words out of Atal's mouth when he entered the room, and he was smiling.

"Greetings, Ancient," I replied as I tried to rise from my supine position.

"Stay as you are, rest. I fear we'll need your strength soon." That was ominous.

"Yes, I suppose Ian told you. Someone betrayed us, tried to have us captured and handed over to Cino. I'm not sure who, but it's important that we find out before they can act."

The ancient elf's eyes gave me a very tired smile. "Unfortunately, attempting to take you was the beginning of their plan; they are already acting. I suspect they wanted to rob the city of your strength and secure you as their weapon."

I frowned; it wasn't like I was that important. "How bad?" I asked simply.

"Four of the villages you fortified have joined the opposition. While I cannot stand their treason, I understand it. Seeing what has happened in recent years, they likely feared for their people. They also know that you were instrumental in bringing down one of their more powerful elders, and they have some of your inventions."

That was bad news. I'd foolishly thought that it was the people I hadn't reached yet that had turned on us, but no, the enemy had let me strengthen their forces before turning their coats. I'd handed over weapons, designs, and secure strongholds—as secure as I could make them. They'd played me, and I'd danced like a stupid monkey for them. Something pinged in my brain though.

"Wait, if they have some of the weapons and tools I've made, they're already close," I muttered.

"Yes, though your escape and some quick responses over the last day or two has likely disturbed their plans. It's possible that their leaders don't know you're back with us, or that we know they're coming. We can't depend on that though. Do you have any ideas?" he asked. "For example, that ability you displayed to Ian, to kill quietly."

"Probably not possible in an open area. Those conditions were very specific. There are a few dangerous things I've been holding onto, but unless they're close and massed . . ." I ran through my mind some of the nastier chemicals I'd stored in my basement—gasses that could kill, flames that would be difficult to extinguish, or even impossible. I had things that would've made governments raise eyebrows in my previous world.

"We'll need to use them if we can."

"How did you learn about their betrayal?" I asked.

"Ah, runners were sent out about a day before you returned. We'd realized you weren't on schedule. I just got word back from some of those still loyal that they were attacked, so we tried to keep runners contained. If they stayed that way or not remains to be seen," he answered.

"Have you verified those reports?" I asked, worried that there might be even more traitors in the mix.

"They are as trustworthy as I can get without going myself. Like you though, I am considering that they may as well be fraudulent." Atal was strangely calm about this. Then again, he was always pretty calm.

"We've got to stop them and soon," I said, rubbing my forehead.

"Yes, we'll need to quickly kill Cino and those closest to him before we can slaughter the rest," Atal said with a nod.

"What if we don't kill the rest? I mean, certainly we'll need to kill the leaders, and anyone even remotely involved with what they're doing to the children. They'll have children of their own though, and those who had no part in this war. If we make an offer of mercy when possible, we might keep them from becoming enemies forever and save at least some lives."

Atal looked at me for a long time. It wasn't clear at first what he was doing, but then I realized he was roaming through his own memories, reliving things that had happened in the past. There were ages behind those eyes, time that I probably couldn't even put into words.

"I forget sometimes that you are so young, Justin," he said. "You have hope that this could work, don't you? That we might allow at least some to survive. I've tried it before, and all it did was lead to more death. I don't think we could, and knowing my reputation, they will never accept it anyway. I've not given any mercy to enemies in a long, long time."

His words pained me. We couldn't keep this up, not as a species. Elves reproduced so slowly, so painfully slowly, that every generation mattered, every life mattered. Between the monsters of this world and accidents, we barely kept our species going, and war like this? It would be impossible to survive if we started using real weapons and participating in real war. It only took one person like Cino to realize that they didn't have to obey the old laws for it all to fall apart.

"Maybe not the men, but the women and children at least?" I asked.

"From my understanding it was a woman who caused the death of your village, was it not? Did her gender make her any less deadly? The children I might consider, but the women? Too many youths like you think them sweet and kind, but there are vipers in that nest, Justin, and if you let them, they'll show you their fangs." He laughed. "Or have you already forgotten the one you helped me kill? Do you not remember her?"

"I do," I admitted. "I just worry that we'll kill ourselves out."

That took his smile away and got me a thoughtful nod. "Indeed, I've worried about such things myself. Though an odd thing to worry about if you've not even tried to make a child with the woman I sent you, isn't it? Certainly, that's something you could work on solving yourself? Or do you prefer the one you had visiting you?"

Him having eyes on both Isha and Ida was worrisome. Was he waiting for something? Would he continue to wait or try something else?

"Ida is a great help, but she wouldn't have a choice if I decided not to give her one. It may be silly in your view, but that bothers me greatly. Keeping others as property bothers me in general," I told him honestly.

"Well keep her, in case your mind should change. I notice you didn't bring up the other woman though, Isha? Trying to keep her from my gaze?" He sat down beside me now, almost laughing.

"I would prefer it if she were left out of things," I said seriously.

"Worry not, child. I won't hurt her." At my continued stare, he shook his head. "I give you my word, not to get to you will I harm the girl. Our enemies might though, so it may do you well to get some protections for her."

"Would you?" I began to ask.

"If you think that I haven't had people watching both you and your home since you came under my purview, you're even younger than I thought," he said, now laughing heartily, a rare and slightly scary thing. "Though do try to keep her close."

"Of course, and thank you."

"You're quite welcome, Justin," he said, making his way to the door. Before he walked out, he turned his head and said, "Now, as soon as you're up to it, get back to making weapons; we need them."

With the war ongoing and getting worse, I was sure he had things to do, things that I didn't need or want to know about. I couldn't organize troops or slay monsters like he could, but maybe I could do enough. The hammer really needed to be finished first, but I couldn't neglect some of the nastier surprises I could bring to the table. If Cino and his people wanted to play, we'd play; and they'd sorely regret bringing themselves up against me.

✦

ANGRY GIRLFRIEND

Before long, I was declared good enough and released into the continuing care of my people. After all, my bones were mended to the extent that I wouldn't be in any immediate danger, and Isha knew some basic healing—at least enough to slowly fix the rest of them.

I quickly headed to my lab. I had a lot of work to do.

"Where exactly do you think you're going?" Isha asked from behind me, looking quite displeased.

"To work," I retorted. "Did you not hear that we need weapons?" I was not willing to be given grief over this.

"We do, but you can't overwork yourself," she chided.

"Isha . . ." I began.

"No. You'll go down there and not wash or eat properly, and then come back up and demand to be healed again," she interrupted.

"I . . . Well, probably."

"Good to see you understand it," she said, poking me in my sore ribs. "I'm going with you."

"You're . . . ?"

"Going with you, to make sure you stop every now and then. Can you take care of things?" she said, turning to the others in the house.

Atie chuckled and nodded. Chien did the same. Ida too made a positive gesture. It surprised me that none of them tried to intervene. Then again, when Chien began laughing too much, Isha fixed him with a glare that made him stop. It seemed she'd taken to keeping the lad in line while I was away.

"Are you not worried there might be trouble?" I asked my aunt, since I knew Chien wouldn't be, and Ida wouldn't say anything about it if she were.

"Hmm? No dear. Ian came by yesterday and told me he's been assigned to help keep an eye on things. With his new strength, he's considered much more important now." There was a sly smile on her lips. The cat who'd caught the canary, I suspected.

"Try not to distract him too much then," I said gruffly before going to my lab, girlfriend in tow.

I had queries about that, but they could wait. How did Ian gain his strength? What was the mechanism and timing? I, of course, knew that almost all elves would experience some magical growth by their hundredth year, but I didn't know why. Was it related to the hair or something else? Maybe the magical growth was even a symptom of something deeper.

There was a lot of research to be done on that front, but I had to ignore it for now. After all, I wasn't a biologist, or a magical theorist. I was a tech guy, and not knowing wouldn't hurt me. If there was a chance to start awakening power in others safely, that might be one thing, but based on what I'd seen, that might be off the table.

I alternated between projects in my lab. Some, like the hammer, required massive quantities of sheer raw power. There was nothing like slamming all your energy into a tiny space just to build a little object and have it drain your magic in a hurry. I switched between these and some less taxing projects, like making chemical weapons.

I'd been hesitant about bringing out the nasty things, but if Cino was coming, and he was—and he wanted to wreck our city and potentially kill hundreds of kids—fuck him. He was getting the worst of chemistry I could manage, and I could manage a lot. Large sealed steel or clay amperes would do as a delivery system, and with the materials I had on hand, they weren't too strenuous to make.

Any chemist, science teacher, or international observer would have been horrified at what I was doing. It was unsafe, and there weren't nearly enough vents, or fume hoods, or protective equipment any-where. Even with all those things, this was borderline mental, but I was desperate and the only thing I could come up with was to turn the Geneva Conventions into a bingo card.

Isha mostly sat in a corner, watching. She didn't bother me when I was working, or ask what I was doing, or why. Her only real input was to interrupt every hour or so, declaring that it was time for a break.

"Food," she said, pointing to something she'd summoned onto a small plate. "And drink."

"Thank you," I said, hoping to assuage any displeasure that might be lingering from the fact that I refused to stop working.

It seemed to work. I wasn't poked or glared at while I ate. The food was simple, basic, but filling and probably nutritious. That thought made me wonder if eating summoned food was good for a person; another question for later. It probably wasn't worse than eating the nearly fake chemical stuff on Earth.

"I have a question," she asked when I finished eating, and before she let me get back to work.

"Oh?" I answered, raising an eyebrow.

"This stuff you're making, can't you just use your fire like you do with the hammer?" she asked, referring to magic in the really old way they had back in the village.

"Yes and no," I answered. "I could make some of it, particularly the fluids and gasses." At her confused look, I clarified. "The stuff that looks like smoke. However, that would be really hard, and I find it a lot easier to break it down with my power and put it back together like I want it."

I'd asked myself the same question once. Water was simple enough to summon, and so were a few other things whose chemical formulas I knew, so long as they were either a liquid or a gas. Solids, on the other hand, were a very different beast. I didn't know why, as the change in state didn't really matter much to me, but that's how it was. Metals were the worst, as they were nearly impossible to simply bring into the world with magic. Making the magical crystal was worse, and it was its own difficult problem.

She accepted my answer, and before long I got back to work, our routine continuing well into the evening. Eventually, though, a more sizable interruption came.

"All right, you're done," she declared as I put one of the vessels down. "It is time to wash, eat dinner, and sleep."

With a shake of my head, I did as she asked, enjoying the quiet end to my day. She even joined me when I went to bed, cuddling up close, but she turned her back when I tried anything more.

"I'm tired from having to watch over an overgrown child all day," she pouted.

"And how long are you planning to continue doing that?" I asked. A day or two more of her supervising me would be funny, but it would also get old fast.

"Until he can learn to keep a schedule."

"Need to build a clock," I grumbled, thinking back to my terrible work habits in my previous life.

"Whatever that is." She didn't even bother to ask.

CHAPTER 40

CINO

Cino

"Beloved forefather," one of my men said, coming to the little hut I'd taken as my own.

"Speak."

"The hunters you sent out did not return with their quarry," he explained.

"Did they return at all?" I asked. Unclear information lost us lives, lives we couldn't afford.

"No, beloved forefather."

"Then they are dead." It was the simple conclusion.

Those men were among my better units, so if they'd not come back, either they had died, or they would die. Things didn't really change though; plans didn't alter just because one man hadn't been caught. It was a shame though; having someone capable of coming up with many new things among my people would have been useful.

"Is something wrong?" asked the girl, Cala, as she tried to cuddle up to me.

"Be silent," I responded, and though she frowned, she obeyed.

This one was . . . useful. Young Cala had been the one to tell me of the pool, of the ones who'd discovered it and what it did. She also gave us valuable information about how to cross the mountains, all for her revenge. Perhaps without her we would have failed in this invasion, been unable to take Atal or its people. Even if we were winning, we were still taking horrible losses, losses we'd not been able to survive without all of our young soldiers.

That said, she was also swiftly outliving her usefulness. She was demanding, annoying, and trying to use me for her own revenge over someone she actually cared for. The only reason I'd not disposed of her already was that I'd had her so many times she might well be with child, and the idea of killing one of my own disgusted me.

After the birth—for there would certainly be one at some point—I'd need to take care of that. Perhaps she could be kept as a pet? Or would it be better to just kill her? Drowning her in that little pool seemed ironic enough to me, or force-feeding her the liquid and leaving her somewhere remote to let it run its course. There were a number of options. Which would I choose?

"Find out what happened if you can. If this Justin has returned to Atal, we should know," I instructed the warrior, who made a gesture of respect before turning to leave.

"Do you think this child will be of use?" asked one of the leaders of my men.

"Perhaps, perhaps not. His inventions have already cost us several of our people, as has his ability. Perhaps it is better to think of him as an elder than a child. Not yet a threat to me, but certainly something to recruit. At any rate, we can keep him and make him work for us. Just getting what he's already displayed could be helpful."

Atal's people were doing things we'd never seen. Particularly with these new metals and things. If I could use those, bring them to my own people, we could expand quickly. These changes would allow me to travel to the far north, to the high mountains and their rulers and bring them to heel, or to the east and the forests that made this thicket look like grass. This Cala may be a toy, but the ruler of the tree villages, that was a woman I would love to have at my side.

"I don't see the point in all these buildings. Won't they have to leave when the herds do?" he asked, indicating the little village.

"The rains are not so damaging here. These people need not move as much either, as the animals here do not migrate as much. You've never left the plains, have you?" I asked, trying to reach through my memories; at this point, it took some time.

"No, beloved forefather. I can't say I much like this place though, the bugs, the strong monsters, and odd foods."

That made me smile. He was right. The monsters upon the plains were nothing compared to some of the things we were seeing here, save for the herd leaders, and they were unlikely to hunt someone. This was a place of easy meat and open running, not for building.

In my youth, we'd hardly even used stone tools, instead preferring working and shaping bones. Large rock faces of the right types were not so common, and with little wood to speak of on the plains, handles were also hard to come by. Over time, though, we'd managed to trade, traveling away from the hunting grounds to the sheer rock faces and getting new ideas. This is also why I wanted that inventor, for I'd seen how good the changes could be.

"There is no need to fret, my child," I answered. "Soon enough the drought should end, the herds return, and then we can return. Some will have to stay to keep our new lands under control, but if you truly object, then you need not be among them."

With my part said, I rose and left the tent. It was time to check on the fighters. To my left, far off through the jungles, were the mountains, and on the other side of them, my beloved home. To my right, not so far that I couldn't smell it, was the sea—a vast, if salty, mass of water. All around me were the walls built by our enemies to keep us away, which now served to keep them contained, restrained.

I made my way to the top of one of those walls now, joining some of my soldiers.

"Have we had any problems?" I inquired.

"No, beloved forefather. This weapon . . ." One of them indicated a large wooden and metal contraption. "It's sufficient to keep the curious beasts at bay. Is there a way to acquire more of them?"

A smile found my lips as I thought about that question. "Perhaps. Will they be difficult to move with us when we make the final push?"

"No, sir," one of the operators answered. He wasn't one of mine, but a local. "Though he was loyal. so he would do well with us."

"Good, good," I nodded. "It won't be long now."

CHAPTER 41

✧

IAN

Ian

"You're returning?" my grandfather asked.

"Yes, the ancestor wants me around in case something else should happen," I answered in a serious tone.

"Be careful, my boy. New strength is often difficult to deal with. Take care not to harm anyone by accident."

I nodded assent and left. It was good advice, as the sudden burst in my power had been astounding. I could now run faster, jump higher, lift things I'd never been able to before. It was a full improvement; even my skin was harder, like that of one of the beasts of the world.

The trip wasn't long, and as I approached my destination, I could see the watchers where they were stationed, quietly keeping an eye on the goings on in the area. Justin hadn't been told, but nearly no one knew he was still alive, and we were keen to keep it that way. It would be best if the enemy didn't know where he was, leaving him to do what he did best, make dangerous things.

"I'm here," I said as I came to the door, which was soon opened by one of my favorite people in the world.

Atie pulled me inside before wrapping her arms around me and burying her face in my chest. Slowly, carefully, I returned the gesture, letting the tips of my fingers rub along her skin.

"Was wondering when you'd get back. Perhaps we should ask Justin to let you stay?" she said invitingly.

"You know I need to return to my family now and then, and attracting more attention here now would be bad. How are you, by the way?"

"I'm well," she chimed. "Thank you for the deliveries. We needed the food, and the two craftsmen have been moaning about getting enough supplies."

"Of course, if you need anything else just ask," I told her, looking down into her beautiful eyes as we stood there together.

She broke our embrace and led me to the little sitting area where she was working on something involving plant fibers. I didn't recognize exactly what it was, but if it was important, I'm sure she'd let me know. Nearby, Ida was doing something similar with a large web of them.

"I can go to the market myself," Atie told me.

"Naturally you could, but for now, please let me or one of the others take care of it." Perhaps she knew that she was being kept away from the public for protection; perhaps not, but there was no need to point it out. "How is he, by the way?"

"How he always is when he gets like this, Ian. At least after Isha's little fit, he's coming back up now and then and sleeping enough. Don't even think he knows what's going on most of the time."

"That's probably for the best, love. We need him working, not worrying about what is coming. It wouldn't help anyway, but his weapons will. Do you know what he has, or when it will be ready?" These were all questions I had to ask, as I was now one of his assigned protectors. Atal knew I was trustworthy with this assignment, at least.

"He said many were done, but he's keeping them in storage until the time comes. Not sure what he made, and he won't explain, but apparently it's nasty stuff."

"Damn right it is," said a male voice as he entered the room. "I don't want to mess with anything that *has* to be stored in steel."

Chien appeared in the room, sweat layering his brow and body, and his clothes were covered with soot. He was getting older and stronger by the day and was likely formidable in his own right. Justin may be odd, but he was a terror, and anyone he trained was guaranteed to be the same. A whole cave of powerful warriors dead, and he didn't even look like he was trying. They just died, like it was nothing. Not to mention the fact that he'd stood before one of the most powerful of the enemy generals and not only survived but managed to turn the fight against her.

"On that note, the other craftsmen are complaining that they're unable to match your quality. Are you holding something back?" I asked Chien.

"No, why would I? If I had to guess from what I've seen, they just aren't getting it hot enough, and that's their problem, not mine. And just so you know, I'm not going to help them. I've got enough going on as it is." He poured himself a cup of water as he spoke, drinking deeply.

I believed him too. Chien had been an annoying little brat all those years ago, working for whoever he could, to get as much as he could, but now he was maturing nicely.

"No worries, I'll make sure you're unbothered by them."

He scoffed. "Bet you could too." At my lack of response, he shook his head. "I forget you can't see it. Atie can't either, can she? If you were strong before . . . Well, be careful. Wouldn't want to see what Justin would do if you ripped his poor auntie in half, or left her unable to walk for days."

I frowned. I was really getting tired of people telling me to 'be careful' like I didn't already know.

"Why wouldn't I be able to . . ." I saw her face as realization struck. "Aren't you too busy to bring that kind of talk in here?" she said, clearly seething.

"Actually, I'm here to see Ida." He turned to the girl in question, where she was quietly working. "Did you manage to finish it?"

She tossed him a piece made of leather and plant fibers that looked like it went over the hand.

"There you are," she said, also clearly unamused by his joke.

"Thank you. Now if you'll excuse me."

He left, and I spent most of the rest of the day, and well into the evening, there. This was a job I enjoyed—spending time with people I cared for, making sure they'd see tomorrow. When she was done with her work, Atie came to where I was sitting and curled up, falling asleep beside me.

For a time, I even entertained the idea of taking her up on her offer. I could stay with them, learn with them, work with them. Day after day, I could stay with this woman I cared for, needing nothing more than that. Perhaps when the war was over . . .

CHAPTER 42

BATTLE BEGINS

The day began like so many others, with the opening of the gates. Not long into the morning, though, something changed. A small group, apparently traders from some village, approached, with goods held on their backs as they made their way forward. None of the guards were familiar with the ten men.

Luckily, the gate guards had been warned. They were told that there might be treachery, some attempt at infiltrating the city. They'd been told, in no uncertain terms, that they were to carefully examine anyone they didn't know. The group, all men of fighting age and with large packs, made their hackles rise.

It was a good thing too, for as soon as they sensed the game was lost, the attempted infiltrators attacked. By the end of it, the ten invaders lay dead, surrounded by triple the number of guards. They'd managed to hide their inner fire, suppressing it until it was nearly invisible. If not for the quick reaction of some of the elder guardsmen, the gate might have fallen, but instead, disaster was averted.

Emergency flares were sent up, pulsing beacons of light. Some of the women who'd gone out to gather made it back before the attack began, but soon the flares had to be changed. Once it became clear that calling people back would only put them in danger, they were told to run, to hide, to survive the coming battle.

While this all happened, I was still in my workshop, deep in concentration. The last of the final touches being put upon my hammer. There came a pounding from the door above, a series of knocks that told me something was terribly wrong.

I bounded up the stairs to find a horrified looking Chien. "Flares, lots of flares," he told me.

"Where's Ian?"

"Here!" the man said, running in the front door.

"We'll need some soldiers to help move the weapons to the walls. Have the girls go to your grandfather's place, in the old tunnel I built. It won't be clean or pleasant, but it's underground and likely the safest place in the city." Then I turned back to my assistant. "Chien, you're with me. We need to get the weapons up here. Wait, what about your family?"

In truth, I knew nothing about Chien's family, other than the fact that his mother was still alive. He didn't like talking about it, and though I'd inquired, she didn't come around.

"She'll be fine; what do you need?" Flippant or not, I didn't have time to argue.

"Come, I'll explain as we move." He followed me to my laboratory, somewhere not even he was used to being. "We need to get these upstairs so the soldiers can take them, and while we do, I'll explain. They're easy to use, just throw, high and far—these first, then those," I said, pointing at two differing sets of symbols. "They need to burst when they land, but absolutely not before."

"Got it," he said, mimicking my use of magic to pull them upstairs and into the courtyard.

Between loads, I looked at my workbench. It sat there like it was waiting, watching. The hammer I'd crafted from iron and solidified magic almost hummed, shimmering in the light. I reached out and placed my fingers around the handle. It was lighter than I'd expected, though with the amount of kinetic magics bound up in it, that shouldn't be too odd. It could move in practically any direction if magic was applied, and should do so very well. Taking the hoop on the handle, I attached it to my belt, ready to hand it off to Atal the moment I saw him. This would be his weapon, one that might actually survive him.

Soldiers were quick to appear, led by Ian. With a few curt words, I sent him and Chien to the far gate with half the bombs. I took the other half to the place that was currently under siege. We needed to be ready if there was some deception; it was pretty much a guarantee.

"Be careful with those," I told the dozen or so men with me. "If you drop one, you're a dead man." Each was carrying a pair of my projectiles, and all were pale when I informed them.

It wasn't absolutely true; the canisters were more durable than that, but if there was a mistake, I wouldn't want to be near one. We hurried through the streets. People were running around in chaos, some trying to make their way to whatever location they were told to defend, others seeking shelter. Everyone was worried and confused. Mothers pulled children inside and close, fear written on their faces.

When we finally arrived, what I saw did not look like what humans believed to be a medieval siege. There was no accounting for the power that was magic, the power to bend the world to your will. Choruses sang, spinning shields and constructions into place; and warriors were walking artillery, spear after spear hefted at the enemy like rounds from a rail-gun. Several mages were atop the walls, tossing balls of fire or force at the enemy, and that was just what I could see from the ground. My ears picked up the crews of the ballistae, firing bolt after bolt in a series of twangs.

Immediately, I made my way to the walls. There was a staircase nearby, and guards didn't dare try to stop me. My steel canisters were left at the bottom, with only a word and pointed finger telling the soldiers where to leave the others.

What I found as I mounted the walls was a swarm, and it was still forming as more poured from the trees. Man after man slipped from the forest and began to pile up, not stopping as they began their attack. Some of their weapons were much like ours. There were staff-slings, designs I'd given over to seemingly loyal villages, along with a few copper and iron spears, though not many.

Their real advantage was magic. The city of Atal was larger than their force, but they'd brought over a hundred of their sacrificial shock troopers, children with burning auras. Most stayed in the back, but who knew how long that would last. For now, they were peppering us with fire, mostly small bolts hurled at wide arcs.

Our leader was nowhere to be seen, but nearby I found someone I recognized.

"Jina!" I yelled as I ran up to her. "Where is your grandfather?"

"At the other walls, you fool! They have your weapons!" As if to punctuate her remark, a man nearby took a ballista bolt to the chest. There was a sickening crack as it pierced him and threw him from the wall, only to come to rest in a bleeding heap down below.

"Not all of them. Is there any way we can get a wind blown out toward the enemy?"

By way of response, she looked at one of the nearby singers, who began to change his tune slightly after nodding. It was subtle, but I could feel it—the change in the direction of the air.

With my magic I reached out, grabbing up several of the nearby canisters as I checked their markings, and then began throwing them. They flew out across the enemy's front line, reaching a peak and then dipping, down, down, until they crashed between the two forces, nearer to the Westers. The enemy army laughed and jeered, a garbled mess that I could only make out at this distance by the tone.

As they were designed to do, each canister broke. Small cracks, enough to let loose the pressurized gas within them. From each of the steel containers clouds of sickly yellow-green mist spread out. The enemy didn't seem bothered or concerned.

"Smoke! You threw smoke at them?!" the healer roared at me, irritated that I'd wasted her time changing the direction of the wind for this.

Then the screaming began.

CHAPTER 43

✦

BATTLE

Chlorine gas was a monster of a thing. While I was a bit limited on exactly what it did, my understanding was that it turned the water found in mucus membranes into hydrochloric acid. Based on the number of elves now clawing at their eyes and grasping their throats in agony, that seemed likely.

When my allies finally tore their eyes from the action, their horrified gazes fell upon me. Several took a step back. Jina looked down at the other canisters, seeming to fear what they might contain. I couldn't blame them. It was unlikely they had any context for what they'd just seen—the monstrous pain dropped upon the enemy.

"Don't stop attacking; keep going!" I told them. There really wasn't time to gawk.

To our enemies' credit, they responded quicker than I thought they would. After only about a minute of flailing in panic, someone used magic to try and start dealing with the harmful gas. It looked like they tried to contest our singers for control of the weather for a moment, before deciding it would be easier to just move the clouds of death away from them. Magic was, after all, a finite resource, and saving what they could was probably important.

It would be more important now, as someone had to heal, or try to heal, the survivors. As soon as the clouds were clear, several people rushed forward, grabbing who they could and pulling them back to their reforming lines. Not even Cino's people wanted to abandon their own to choke on their own blood.

Minutes passed where little other than exchanging fire was over. Our enemy had taken heavy losses to their forward force, losing about a quarter of the people we could see from our vantage point. Sure, some of them would come back, but not all. I took a few shots here and there at people who were trying to evacuate, and at those trying to pull them away. Taking out their healers would be magnificent, if we could manage it.

Between the losses and the fact that the child soldiers were burning themselves out slowly, a siege benefited us more than it did them, and they seemed to know this. Their plan had clearly been to blitz the gate and move into the city, but they had limited options to achieve that now.

The Westers divided the children into two groups, half on the front line and half on the back line, and they sent them moving forward. While the back group upped their fire from a few light shots to a veritable hail of spells, the front line began to work their way forward at increasing speed, pushing themselves above the ground with magic.

Our shielding mages had to duck. Attacks were passing through their shields, since the mages had to conserve their magic, and quickly overwhelming their abilities. They needed to prioritize and pull back their shields, protecting only the siege engines, the casters, and the gate. Other areas of the wall were pelted, and even if the spells weren't massive, there were many. I ducked behind a raised portion of the wall, letting the bolts and arrows hiss and ping around me.

The city wasn't doing well though. Many of these magical hits were flying past us and into nearby houses and businesses, ripping away chunks of wall and the living wood that composed parts of buildings. Anyone caught in the crossfire would suffer terribly.

However, before the charge made it even halfway to us, the storm began to fade. A quick peek from my hiding spot told me why. The child soldiers they were using couldn't handle it; they were dropping like flies. One by one, the back line fell, some shaking and seizing on the ground, some immolating themselves. The others didn't stop, though, too afraid of what would happen if they did.

At that moment, another problem became clear. None of our people were firing upon the charging unit. A few were still attacking the opposing army, but nobody was trying to stop the force marching quickly upon our gate, a gate they couldn't be allowed to get to.

"I'll do it," came the shaky voice of Jina as I began to raise my hand to strike. "This is my duty."

Tears poured down her face as she brought her hands before her. I'd seen her do magic, and on some level I knew that she was incredibly powerful, but this drove the point home. Energy poured into a small ball, about the size of a marble, purple and swirling. She was sweating bullets with the effort of it, but she didn't stop, didn't slow down.

With a final flick of her hand, the healer released what she'd been preparing. The orb shot out, meeting the middle of the pack of charging younglings. There was a silent flash of purple, and as one they fell, eyes sightless, bodies tumbling as they died mid-step, like puppets with their strings cut. Everything in the radius of that baleful burst just died, nothing more, nothing less.

The battlefield froze. For a heartbeat, the only sound that could be heard was the gasping and weeping of the woman beside me. She'd fallen, too, on her hands and knees. Her aura appeared weakened, like she'd used all her power for that one spell, and maybe she had, making sure that those innocents didn't suffer more than they needed to, making sure they came to no more harm than she had to inflict to save others.

The roar of battle doubled, both sides furious at what had happened. The rain of magic stopped as the last of the children burned themselves out, and both sides continued with their bombardment.

Now was the moment, so I used my magic to grab the rest of the containers, huffing as I spent the power I'd kept in reserve to hurl them at the enemy.

Not wanting to deal with gas again, the opposing force swiped them all from the air in a volley of kinetic bolts, shattering the steel containers into nothing but scrap. Our enemy had learned, but not enough. These canisters contained not gas, but liquid—liquid that spent a mere moment appearing as water until it met the air.

The liquid ignited, and our enemies who'd rained magic upon us received a rain of fire in return. Some of them tried to fall to the ground and roll, hoping to extinguish the flames, but it didn't help. A few of them covered parts of themselves completely, making sure no air could get to the fire; that didn't help either. More than one mage had managed to avoid getting drenched and began shooting out water, hoping to douse at least some flames, but it made things worse. releasing a very familiar yellow gas.

Fluorine was scarce, but these rocks held some. The worst part? I knew exactly how to make and store chlorine trifluoride, thanks to my memory of that awful formula. It burned . . . well pretty much anything. Soil, rocks, trees, animals, houses, bridges, glass, ashes, asbestos, and, like I said, pretty much anything else. It couldn't be put out, and I didn't even know how toxic it would be. Even the light spray that much of the enemy army had gotten would be . . . well . . . enough.

The Westers panicked, but it did them no good. Nothing did. Many of their people died screaming. I felt no regret. They'd made their choices. They'd reaped horrors upon us, and now they could suffer the same. They could watch and do nothing as those they cared for perished, as we had—waiting for the flames to go out as we pummeled them with even more death from our walls.

They broke—too tired, too scared, too hurt—and began to retreat to the forest. Before they got far, though, a light began to appear in the trees, a sparking painful blue. What looked like lightning crested over the towering tree line, arcing and snapping. At first I didn't realize what it was, and then it hit me. Our efforts had attracted a bigger fish.

The enemy halted their run away from us and split so that we could see their ancient stride forward onto the field.

Cino had finally arrived.

CHAPTER 44

FALL OF AN ANCIENT

Cino was accompanied by far fewer soldiers than I would have anticipated. Perhaps he felt he needed to stand alone, to display showmanship. I didn't know or care. Much of our fire was redirected at him. Bolts, and spells, and spears bounced off some kind of shield he had up around himself.

In his unit were a few singing along with him, one of which I recognized instantly, even at this distance. Cala. The girl who'd gone to him after leaving Elayatol, who'd told him about the pool and its effects, who'd caused so many terrible things to happen. This war may have been unavoidable, but she'd made it so much worse, caused so much pain.

After observing us for a moment, Cino took a deep breath in.

"WALLS!" someone screamed from nearby. No one hesitated.

Cino screamed, and the ground before him ripped apart, while upon our walls, spellcaster after spellcaster threw up the same type of shield I'd used against the other singer I'd fought. I joined in, of course, a beat behind after realizing what was coming, but still doing my part.

Cino's magic tore layer after layer from the barriers we created, as he moved what seemed to be a rippling column of sound up and down the wall. There was damage, but manageable amounts of it, for it didn't matter how strong his ability was, if it simply couldn't reach us. There was visible shock from his people as his scream subsided. The ancient monster himself looked incredulous. How long had it been since someone had stood up against him?

The ruckus attracted attention, and moments later, a disturbance made its way around the far side of the walls. At first, it was unclear what was going on, merely that there was some kind of roiling mass; but as it came closer, we all got to see. I hadn't realized that the enemy had no physical magic users for this part of the siege, but now it was clear where they were.

It was like watching a flock of starlings fight an eagle as they came into view. Atal stood at the center, with dozens circling him, darting forward to attempt a strike where they could. I watched as he caught an attacker, ripping the man to shreds, but in that second others pulsed in, hitting, striking, aiming for anything they could.

There were too many. In the end, Atal might have been able to win, to beat them down until there weren't enough to divide his attention, but they were wearing away at him. All along his body I could see small cuts and darkening bruises. He was covered in blood, and not all of it his enemies'. If possible, he needed to retreat and heal, to get the weapon I made for him.

"ATAL!" I shouted, hoping to get him to come to me, if only for a second, but he paid no mind.

"Grandfather!" Jina screamed from beside me, she too wanting him to fall back.

No, he wanted this over as much as we did. This seemed to suit Cino fine, as the other ancient shouted a series of orders before taking another breath. I tried to throw a shield around Atal, others did too, but it was in vain.

All the warriors who'd been fighting Atal scattered like roaches before turning toward our wall. In the blink of an eye, they were upon our ranks. Near me, a man covered in scars and blood threw himself forward, catching the stone edge and swinging, club in hand.

I barely had enough time to turn from the fighting rulers and protect myself. I had a mere second to throw a shield between us before he slammed into it, club blurring as he delivered blow after blow upon it. He should have known better though; most of our forces were still fairly fresh.

The warriors who'd had little to do in this fight other than sling stones and deliver ammo to the ballistae were ready. With no magic, they couldn't rain hell upon our enemies, they couldn't kill dozens at a time from so far away, but now that the targets were among us, spears thrust at the intruders, and knives were drawn, as brave men stepped up against those they had no chance of beating alone. They weren't alone, though, weren't separated to keep the mages and the strongest held down. They were in groups that, as one, fell upon the soldiers who had been assaulting Atal.

Half a dozen of these warriors rushed the man who had attacked me, weapons ready. I knew these men in passing, people I'd made weapons or armor for, old friends of Ian's or guards from Atal's palace. One who'd requested a spear from me took a club to the face, his head imploding as the weapon he so valued fell, but those around him didn't falter. Before I could even cast a proper spell to take on my attacker, he was pinned like a butterfly to the wall, three copper and iron points buried in his gut.

I gave them a quick nod, as I turned back to the front, trying to think of how I'd get the weapon to Atal. With something he could actually use, perhaps there was a way for him to gain some ground.

I was wrong. As I looked on, our leader charged at the master of the enemy forces, leapt, and bounced upward. Cino, it seemed, had tricks of his own, an unseen barrier that sent Atal flying.

It was enough. Stripped of his arms, alone, and with nothing to push against with his monumental strength, Atal was vulnerable. He turned in the air and looked regretful, almost sad. He knew what came next.

Cino screamed once more—a tight, concentrated beam of power which slammed right into Atal's chest, sending a spray of gore, blood, and bone, ending the life of one who'd seen so many years.

The fall of Atal didn't end things immediately. Not everyone saw it, and not all who did stopped fighting. Near me, Jina paled, terrified and trembling. Her grandfather, who had served as the rock, the pillar of our community, was now gone, broken and no more.

"ENOUGH!" shouted Cino. Some kind of spell boosted his voice so all could hear him.

He strode forward, as if he hadn't a care in the world, confident that the only one who could truly oppose him now lay dead at his feet. He didn't hurry, didn't rush. He didn't need to. Cino didn't stop until he came within about thirty feet of our gate, with most of his people forming behind him.

"Your master is dead, but you need not die with him. Surrender to me, open your gates, drop your weapons, and some of you may yet be allowed to live under my rule. Refuse and you shall perish, your families shall perish, your friends shall perish. I am done playing."

My mind raced. Could I get my people out? Could we escape? Could I get Isha, Atie, and Ida? What about Chien and Ian? What about some of the others? What about the girls in the street of flowers and the soldiers? Even Jina. Could I save her? She was here with me, but I doubted we could flee in time.

"Fuck it," I declared, reaching a decision. My hand reached down and grasped the handle of the hammer I'd spent so long making. It thrummed in my grasp, responding as if it were part of me, welcoming me, ready.

CHAPTER 45

✦

THE HAMMER FALLS

Jina

We were done. There was nothing else to do, nobody who could win this fight. We'd tried, and we'd lost. Could I flee? Could I escape if I ran now, maybe grabbing a few of my closest and most trusted and running? There was a chance, but I needed to act quickly. I refused to either be slaughtered like a beast or kept as a pet by this monster.

My power was faltering, rebelling against me after what I'd done to those children. In my mind, I knew it to be right, but my heart was pained, and that pain kept my strength from working as it should. No one else should have to carry that burden though. Perhaps, in time my heart would calm, agree with my mind, but right now I was weaker than I'd been since I was under a century old.

"Fuck it," said the boy beside me. He was one of the ones I'd like to flee with, for after the terrors he'd unleashed today, he might be the only one who can come up with something to defeat Cino.

He pulled something off his belt, something I'd not noticed in the heat of battle. It was . . . a mass of magical crystals, formed into the shape of a hammer. Where in the name of all the oceans and seas had he found those! Did he know the rarity? How had he even formed them together like that?

Then he did something I expected even less—he jumped from the wall. There was magic in him as he moved through the air, angling as he raised the weapon above his head, trying to get to just the right place. There was a brief flash as he shoved mana into his construction.

The hammer fell.

Cino

Victory was sweet. Atal was dead. Soon his people would fall at my feet. My territory would grow, as would my influence, the things I could get, the things I could use. This place had so many new creations. I'd be taking them, and the people I wanted. Maybe I'd even stay here a while, rest while I and my men enjoyed the spoils of war.

A youth jumped from the wall. He was no ancient, no elder, just some fool. Good. He would serve as an example to others. There was magic in him, though, enough to angle his approach, unfortunate to lose that. As he grew nearer, he hefted his weapon above his head. It was some kind of hammer, one that would certainly bounce off of my shield. Then there was a burst of light.

The hammer fell.

Cala

I won. This place, these people—they were finished. There was even an added bonus. Though he was hard to make out from here, I could see him—my enemy upon the walls. He hadn't been in Elayatol, of course. He accepted his exile. Nor had we been able to locate him after fleeing capture, the bastard disappearing like smoke on the wind. But he was here now.

The soldiers had told me to stay back as they marched forward behind Cino. I was no fighter, no strong warrior, or powerful user of fire. No, I just helped my lovely Cino where I could. All the things I would do for him tonight when he was done; how I looked forward to it.

As my lover strode up to the walls, I smiled even brighter, for Elian drew a weapon and leapt at him. Cino would rip him to shreds now, here for me and everyone else to see. I would replay this memory in my mind a thousand times.

The fool Elian lifted his hammer above his head, and for an instant, something shone like the sun.

The hammer fell.

Justin/Elian

Holding this weapon was like holding a bolt of lightning in my hand. It felt like it was a part of me, because it was an extension of me. I realized this as I jumped. A quick spell altered my trajectory, slowing my fall and pushing me forward. It would've been most embarrassing to break both my legs doing this and would surely mean my defeat.

There was only one shot, one chance, while this monster felt he'd won. So I took it, determined to win, or die trying. I wrapped my magic around the hammer as I hefted it, and something strange happened.

This hammer wasn't made with the same type of crystal I'd seen Jina use all those years ago. It wasn't a conduit for magic alone; it was magic, *my* magic. The crystals I'd created were made from my magic, but I'd never been able to use them correctly, for I'd never known what I needed them to do, not like this. The hammer drank up the power, and as I lifted it above my head, it burned like a newly forming star. This was my magic, and I'd just given it my intent—to destroy everything in front of me in a single blow.

The hammer fell.

And the world shuddered in response.

My weapon didn't strike, it atomized. This thing I'd built was made of pure magic, pure kinetic force, and force it became. In a flash, everything but the scraps of iron that once made up the handle simply ceased to be, as did everything in the direction of my swing.

Cino must have had some kind of shield around him because there was a look of panic on his face before the barrier before him was shattered, and he became nothing but a splash of red mist. From there, the blast went outward in a wave of destruction and death. The ground rippled and buckled as it was scorched.

Even though the angle was wide, the destruction was still astounding. There was no grass left before me for a hundred feet. Vegetation at the edge of the tree line toppled and fell, with some near them thrown like rag dolls from the blast.

It lasted only a moment, but when it was over, nobody was standing. I had to pick myself off the ground; the mangled chunk of steel in my hand was all that was left of the hammer. Luckily, magic didn't have to follow the rules of physics all the time, so there'd been no backblast. Behind me, the city wall still stood, the defenders still perched atop it, unsure what to do.

I knew what I had to do though. I walked forward through the land destroyed by my strike, upon barren ground and past uprooted foliage and rocks. I walked past the charred and ruined remains, the places where men had died from spells, or siege engines, or gas, or fire. I walked back to where the woods began. It seemed such a small distance from where our enemies had emerged.

I found her there, crawling on the ground, legs bent and broken where the very edge of my attack had struck her, among broken branches and toppled trees, still somehow alive, somehow conscious.

"Hello, Cala," I said.

"You!" she spat, turning. "Why won't you die?!"

"I've got better things to do. You, on the other hand, have done more than enough."

With a flick and a flash of power, I pulled together the pieces of the hammer's handle, twisting and melting them into a crude spike. It was ugly, but that fit its purpose. Seeming to sense my intent, Cala panicked, trying to pull herself away, but the effort was useless with broken legs.

Flipping her over on her back, I knelt on her stomach as she clawed and bit at me, small hands ripping at anything she could. She'd spent years as the kept woman of some tyrant, though, while I'd spent those same years shaping metal. She had neither the skill nor the strength to stop me as I plunged my spike into her chest.

I stabbed her for all the suffering she'd caused. I stabbed her for the dead children she'd helped create. I stabbed her for the villages destroyed. I stabbed her for the soldiers who'd lost their lives defending their homes. I stabbed her for the innocents. I stabbed her for my parents. I stabbed her for Isha's family. I stabbed her for Elaya. I stabbed her for Ninden. I stabbed her for Larus. I stabbed her for my people. I stabbed her for my home. I stabbed her for showing Cino the pool. I stabbed her because I shouldn't have even shown her. I stabbed her because I didn't stop her when she first left our village. I stabbed her because it was my fault. I stabbed her without realizing I was weeping. I stabbed her because I should never have let this happen. I stabbed her without realizing I was weeping. Again, and again, and again, and again, until I couldn't anymore.

When my strength finally failed, and I was no longer able to lift the spike, what lay below me was a pile of gore. So, once more I rose and walked, this time back to the gate. The people there were gawking at me, afraid. They opened the gate back up and just stood around watching me as I stumbled through.

"I'm done," I told them, before finding a corner to collapse in.

EPILOGUE

✦

S o, are you sending someone to kill me?" I asked. "Or are you going
to try and put me on a throne?"

Jina and Shorin looked uncomfortable. They represented the council of elders who were now in charge of Atal. The city's name had remained the same—a sort of memorial to the fallen elder.

"Neither," Shorin said. "We know you saved us. Everyone knows what would have happened if Cino had taken the city, and nobody would dare harm you for that. The thing is . . ."

"You're terrifying!" Jina interjected. "Those things you used against his army, that's scary, too scary. You're also too young to rule. There's not a single pale hair on your head, child. Nobody would respect you as a leader. The other ancients wouldn't accept it either. One or more of them would decide you were a joke and try to do something about it." Jina really had a way with words.

"So what then?" I asked.

"Well, we spoke, and there are a few options," Shorin began. "There is one thing we'd like to . . . request of you. You see, two ancients have died, and that's no small thing. Tradition dictates that we send a messenger out to let the others know. If you went . . . it would allow plenty of time for things to calm down here, and you've already demonstrated you're skilled enough to travel." Shorin looked nervous as he spoke, stuttering a bit as he requested something he really shouldn't.

"You're exiling me," I said.

"No, you'll be able to come back," Jina said lazily. "We're allowing time for you to grow and for our people's fear to subside."

"Fine," I told them.

"J-just like that?" Shorin asked, confused.

"Just like that. This isn't the first time I've been exiled, and to be honest, I don't like seeing people cringe every time they see me. I'll add to that the fact that I'd really like to get away for a while, see something new. Just to be clear, though, I do plan on returning."

That evening, I gathered my people together.

"I'm going away for a while. There's a message that needs to be taken to the other ancients, and I've been chosen as the messenger, for a lot of reasons. Of course, I want you to know that I love you all, and I'll be back when I can."

"Not alone," Isha said. "I'm going too."

"Isha . . ." I began.

"Do I need to go get something to shut you up with?" she asked sweetly.

"Fine." If Isha came with me, it would make the trip better at least.

"Yeah, I'm coming too, boss. Never gone wrong sticking with you, and you can't get rid of me that easy," Chien said with a shrug and a laugh.

"All right, anyone else?"

"Ian and I are . . . together now," Auntie Atie demurred. "I'd offer but . . ."

"Stay then. Mind keeping an eye on the house for me?" I'd already cleaned out my lab this afternoon, purging it of anything dangerous.

"Of course!" she said with a smile.

"Do you mind if I stay too?" Ida asked.

"Ida, you've always been free to stay or leave as you wish. Just try not to cause Atie problems okay?"

She nodded, before going back to being silent. I guess old habits die hard.

Chien

I was leaving, something I had no compunctions about, but there was one thing I had to do first. I made my way into the back streets, toward the Street of Flowers, ignoring the girls as they flirted, picking my way along until I found what I was looking for, the place where I'd been born.

As I walked in, none of the girls even bothered looking at me; they all knew better. I strode up to the owner, where she sat in the main reception area.

"Is she here?" I asked.

"Yes, in her room, and alone for now," she told me, polite, but cold. I couldn't blame her for her icy tone; I'd left her employ many years ago.

I tossed her something for her troubles and made my way into the brothel proper, deep into one of the innermost rooms.

"Hello, Mother," I said.

"Oh, it's you," she replied, looking me up and down. She was sober, so that was good. It meant she might remember what I had to tell her. "Did you bring me anything?"

She always did that—always asked for more, more to feed her habit. The fermented berry wine she liked so much wasn't easy to come by, and she had it far too often. I could even see it in her face, the rose color that never went away.

"No, I came to tell you I'm leaving the city, for a long time. You'll have to take care of yourself from now on."

She stood, angry, and stomped toward me. "I don't need you to take care of me, Chien. I've been taking care of myself longer than you know."

"Good," I agreed, and turned to leave.

"You rude brat!" she roared, and moved to slap me.

I let her. I'd put up a wall of force between myself and her hand. It did nothing, at least to me. She fell back cradling her fingers.

"I'm leaving," I informed her again, this time quite coldly. "Try to be safe while I'm gone."

"Your little 'boss' isn't your father, boy!" she spat, trying to hurt me.

"Maybe not, but he's been a better father to me than you've ever been a mother." I left her to think on that, not caring about anything else she had to say.

ABOUT THE AUTHOR

Wandering Agent is the North Carolina–based author of the Melody of Mana and Elevation of Mana series as well as other fantasy and isekai stories.

Podium
DISCOVER
STORIES UNBOUND
PodiumAudio.com

www.ingramcontent.com/pod-product-compliance
Lightning Source LLC
Chambersburg PA
CBHW020656120726
47906CB00001B/288